MALA VIDA

MALA VIDA

A Novel

MARC FERNANDEZ

Translated from the French by
MOLLY GROGAN

ARCADE PUBLISHING · NEW YORK

First English-language Edition

First published in French under the title *Mala Vida* by the Librairie Générale Française

This is a work of fiction. Names, places, characters, and incidents are either the products of the author's imagination or are used fictitiously.

Arcade Publishing books may be purchased in bulk at special discounts for sales promotion, corporate gifts, fund-raising, or educational purposes. Special editions can also be created to specifications. For details, contact the Special Sales Department, Arcade Publishing, 307 West 36th Street, 11th Floor, New York, NY 10018 or arcade@skyhorsepublishing.com.

Arcade Publishing® is a registered trademark of Skyhorse Publishing, Inc.®, a Delaware corporation.

Visit our website at www.arcadepub.com.

10 9 8 7 6 5 4 3 2 1

Library of Congress Cataloging-in-Publication Data

Names: Fernandez, Marc, author. | Grogan, Molly, translator.
Title: Mala vida : a novel / Marc Fernandez ; translated from the French by Molly Grogan.
Other titles: Mala vida. English
Description: First English-language edition. | New York : Arcade Publishing, 2019.
Identifiers: LCCN 2018026310 (print) | LCCN 2018027053 (ebook) | ISBN 9781628727463 (ebook) | ISBN 9781628727432 (hardcover : alk. paper)
Classification: LCC PQ2706.E754 (ebook) | LCC PQ2706.E754 M3513 2019 (print) | DDC 843/.92—dc23
LC record available at https://lccn.loc.gov/2018026310

Cover design by Studio LGF
Cover photograph: Shutterstock

Printed in the United States of America

For Lea and Diego, naturally . . .

"I know that if we don't pay attention to the past, one day the past will pay attention to us."

—JOYCE CAROL OATES

"The future torments us, the past holds us back; this is why the present escapes us."

—GUSTAVE FLAUBERT

MALA VIDA

MALA VIDA

PROLOGUE

FRANCO MAY BE dead; his supporters live on. The electorate has a short memory, which a forty-five-year-long dictatorship could not jog, and the voters have passed the baton to a new leader, who will beat them with it again if necessary. Even seniors, the generation that endured years of privation, hunger, and submission under Franco, voted overwhelmingly in favor of the Alliance for a Popular Majority, the APM. Looking grief-stricken, the Socialists' interior minister has just confirmed the polls' predictions: a decisive victory for Franco's cronies. Diego is no fool. The APM's faithful are celebrating on a stage erected in front of party headquarters; they're young and neatly dressed, and not a single one is old enough to have been alive during the Franco years. Behind the scenes, however, Franco's old bigwigs are there, pulling strings from the shadows, lulling those partiers on stage into the lie that they are the ones calling the shots.

Harboring no illusions but acting rather out of a sense of duty, Diego waited until nearly the last minute to vote, just when the polling stations were about to close. Like most of his fellow citizens, he doesn't have a shred of confidence in politicians anymore, but his rule is hard and fast: vote, no matter what. And yet, this time, he came as close as he ever has to breaking it. Women and men fought so he could cast a ballot. He went straight home to his apartment in the Malasaña neighborhood, Madrid's Soho. He kept his telephone off; he was in no mood to discuss an inevitable fascist victory with his colleagues, who were sure to call to prod him for a pseudo-post-election analysis. He had downloaded the final episodes of the HBO series *True Detective,* and with his laptop on his knees, a bottle of vodka, and some Schweppes at arms' reach, he fell quickly into a restless sleep. That is until he awoke with a start, and curiosity took over.

He turns on the TV to watch the catastrophe unfold live. It's the same scene on every station: stone-faced anchors who know they are making their last appearance on the nightly news before a massive media reshuffle, APM officials grinning from ear to ear and showing off for the cameras, no longer even bothering to hide their disdain for the losers, already.

Night has fallen. A night, Diego tells himself, that will last four years, the length of the new government's term of office. A live feed from the Plaza de Cibeles, where Real Madrid celebrates its victories (or did, before FC Barcelona relegated them, for what seems like forever, to second place), jolts him out of his torpor. On the flat screen, the usual crowd of victorious supporters wait for the APM's leaders to arrive. Dozens, even hundreds, of people are belting out the Spanish national anthem and waving red-and-yellow flags. A detail catches Diego's eye: Franco's coat of arms, displayed on many of the flags. Outlawed since El Caudillo's death, it's back, even before the official results have been announced. It's going to be pure hell.

At the very back of the crowd where the television cameras can't reach them, groups of skinheads wearing Real Madrid scarves are making the Nationalists' raised-arm salute. Real's hooligans, the Ultras Sur, are right at home here. Not far away, an assembly of black-cloaked clergy watches the scene play out, wry smiles curling their lips. The Church did its part, of course, to call its flocks out to vote APM. All of the most explosive elements of society are there: the Francoists, the far right, Opus Dei . . . a ticking time bomb. Meanwhile, modern Spain gasps its last breath, live on television, and with it go progressive values, gay rights, and tolerance.

Time for another vodka tonic. Diego pours himself a drink without moving from the couch. As he returns the bottle to the floor, his gaze catches on a framed photo on the TV console. He picks it up slowly, looks at it for a long minute, and hugs it to himself before putting it gently back in its spot. He throws his cocktail back, a tear on his cheek.

Ribbons of smoke scroll from the half-opened window of a car parked a few streets from the Plaza de Cibeles. A trembling hand emerges to toss a cigarette stub to the sidewalk. Sitting behind the wheel for hours, she has smoked an entire packet of Fortuna and listened to Manu Chao's *Clandestino* for the hundredth time. "I am the outlaw"—a subliminal message to steel her for what she has to do next.

Wait for the precise moment. Take deep breaths. Rehearse what to do. Killing a man is never easy. The morning edition of *El País* is lying on the passenger seat. Under it lies a pistol, waiting for its owner to put it to good use. A Walther P38 that she bought yesterday in a downtown gun store. She didn't make any pretense about it. What would be the point? Her plan goes into action in just a few minutes. This goddamn election night is finally going to end. Eventually, they'll all head home, all these fascists. Her target, too. She has been following him for weeks. There isn't anything about this young APM city councilman that she doesn't already know. At the tender age of thirty-six, he's one of the right's rising stars, guaranteed a cushy cabinet position after today's results. She knows he'll never enjoy his new privileges. A single bullet to the head, just one, is the only thing waiting for him, far from the Treasury Department.

Another cigarette. She strokes the grip of the pistol to relax. Closing her eyes, she takes a deep drag, runs her hand through her long, dark hair and smoothes the collar of her blouse. Applause in the distance startles her: the future prime minister has finished his speech. Not much time left. She opens her eyes and looks in the rearview mirror. The empty street won't be empty much longer. Before long, the evening's victors will be flooding it as they begin to make their way home. She'll have to act quickly. She starts the car and shivers from the burst of AC that hits her.

Finally, identically dressed families of APM supporters are streaming into the street. The men are in checkered shirts, their hair neatly parted to one side, sweaters draping their shoulders. The women are in sensible skirt suits with strings of pearls at the neck. Three, four, sometimes five children follow behind them. There are men in suits who are high-fiving skinheads in leather jackets. At the subway station, they go their separate ways, fists brandished in victory. Some will take public transportation home; others go looking for their cars parked at a safe distance from the celebrations. They'll have to bide their time in traffic jams. Money has no smell, they say, and the far right will take anyone's vote, rich or poor.

Eventually the street empties, and silence returns. She has time for three or four more cigarettes, but in a fit of nerves, she puts each one out half-smoked.

She waits a full thirty minutes more for her target to finally appear. Paco Gómez is alone. He walks slowly, with his tie in one hand, cell phone in the other. He is answering the dozens of texts he has received over the course of the evening. They are all congratulatory messages. The new cabinet will be announced tomorrow, and the jackals are already circling.

With his eyes still fixed on his phone, he approaches the car. She waits for him to pass her slightly. Then, slowly, she reaches her hand out the window she was careful to leave half-opened and aims for the back of his head.

1

"THE TIME IS midnight. Thank you for listening to Radio Uno. It's Friday, which means Diego Martin is up next after the news with *Radio Confidential*."

A commercial plays. He's on in five. Diego arrives at the studio at the last possible moment carrying an armload of files, just like he always does. He's also dangling a cigarette between his lips, although smoking is not allowed in the studio. He takes a certain pleasure every week in this small violation of the laws that be, this raised middle finger to the sterile society ushered in six months ago by the APM's victory in the national elections, which plunged the country into a terrifying stupor. At any rate, it's a small risk he's taking. Plus, it's the weekend. The chances of running into anyone between his minuscule office on the sixth floor and the tiny broadcast studio on the first basement level where his producer is waiting for him are slim. There's no room for him in the main studio on the ground floor where the morning shows are broadcast and the station's star anchors work. Even if they had offered it to him, he would have refused; he could never do his show in a room named after Escrivá de Balaguer, the founder of Opus Dei. Changing the name of the legendary Ortega y Gasset studio was one of the first moves, and it was a highly symbolic one, made by the public radio station's new director after the APM's win. It was proof of the government's stupidity and the influence of the Catholic Church in the halls of power.

Public broadcasting took a beating in the post-election media purge. Program directors thought to be in bed with the Socialists were shown the door. Anchors too critical of the APM were let go. Journalists judged dangerous by the new government were fired. So long. Farewell. Adios. All of them invited to take a hike to wherever the Socialist rose grows, to sign up for unemployment or to vent their anger on a blog that no one will read. Gone, all of them, except Diego. And he knows full well that he owes his job to the same government that is flirting blithely with everything Francoist, reactionary, and retrograde. The government's spokesperson said as much in a press conference: "You can hardly accuse us of a media takeover. Look, Diego Martin is still on *Radio Uno*, and he's not exactly what you'd call an APM supporter, to say the least." So take that!

The on-air light above the studio door is still off. In a tiny booth next door, the newsreader is apathetically intoning the latest headlines, sports, and weather. Diego is in his chair now, headphones perched on one ear, opened files spread out around him. A plastic cup with a finger of cold dispenser coffee sits at the ready to serve as an impromptu ashtray but looks as if it could spill onto his papers at any moment. Visible through the glass separating the studio and the control room, the producer is mad as hell.

"Jesus Christ, Diego! You're a goddamn pain in the ass with your cigarette. It screws up the equipment!"

"It's either that or radio silence, amigo—your choice. I've been doing the same thing for twenty years, and I'm not going to change now. You know, it's you reformed smokers who are the royal pain in the ass. You're the worst anti-cigarette bigots there are. You'd have been better off not quitting!"

They are interrupted by Nancy Sinatra singing "Bang Bang (My Baby Shot Me Down)," the title song of *Radio Confidential*, lifted from the soundtrack of *Kill Bill*.

"Good evening, night prowlers," Diego intones, launching his two-hour weekly show with his usual greeting. "Ahead tonight, my exclusive report on the LAPD. I spent a week embedded with Los Angeles's finest. I'll take you on night patrol and behind the scenes with the City of Angels's homicide detectives. While I was there, I also interviewed one of the greatest crime fiction writers today, a controversial personality and an undeniable literary talent, Mr. James Ellroy, in person. But before we get started, it's the moment I know you've all been waiting for: the weekly courtroom chronicle of our anonymous, now famous magistrate. Friends, I give you our very own Prosecutor X!"

This opener to his show—an idea that came to Diego just after the APM's win—has been a huge success since it launched. It is also the most downloaded three minutes on Radio Uno's website, to the enormous frustration of the station's executives. The national and international public that tunes in weekly live or via podcast to the chronicler's biting sallies has no idea who Prosecutor X is. His voice is masked to keep his identity a secret.

Week after week, this perfectly informed insider pulls back the curtain on the contradictions of power as exercised by the judiciary. He also reports on cases currently before the courts and on investigations into the activities of APM members and their cronies, usually buried by unscrupulous colleagues working under orders from the attorney general.

In fact, Prosecutor X has broken so many scandals that the government has launched a veritable manhunt to uncover his identity. All have been unsuccessful so far. To be sure, Diego and his mystery guest spare no precaution to keep their secret safe. They never speak by phone or email. Instead, thumbing their noses at the criminals they are discussing on the show or investigating, they have taken a page out of the book of the Sicilian mafia and communicate via *pizzini*, those bits of paper the Godfather uses to deliver his instructions. Prosecutor X handwrites the week's report in one or two paragraphs, and a courier—the only person Diego trusts—picks it up and delivers it to the journalist. What no one outside this unusual threesome knows is that it is the courier who reads the report, recording it the day before the show airs.

Prosecutor X drops a bombshell tonight. Yet another. The president of the region of Valencia, Spain's third largest city, has taken kickbacks from local construction companies in exchange for government contracts. That old trick. Not only has he built himself a new house for next to nothing, but he's also received a number of gifts ranging from designer suits to trips and even a yacht. A yacht! In sum, this elected official hasn't spent so much as a penny on clothes, food, accommodation, or even to go on vacation, for years.

Diego can't stop grinning as the chronicle airs. The show's producer, on the other hand, who is hearing the news for the first time, wonders how much longer he'll be working the control booth. Two of his colleagues have already been fired in the last six months.

Prosecutor X wraps up: "Will this scandal, or rather this perfect storm of scandals, be enough to force his resignation? Not a good bet in this country where, for the last several months, impunity has become the order of the day."

The show follows its usual progression over the next two hours. The running order sheet alternates stories, the main interview, and musical breaks: nothing fancy, but it does the job. The final minutes are reserved for a listener call-in, live and unedited. Most callers are supportive; others just want to insult Diego, usually calling him a "Commie journalist." Occasionally, he hears from listeners posing as informers—snitches, more like—who rat on their neighbors and family. Diego insists on giving them all airtime, a tricky exercise at times, but he has a knack for cutting them off when they go too far and for talking reason to the worst conspiracy theorists.

"It's two a.m., time to wish you goodnight. Thanks to everyone out there listening. See you next week if all goes well, same time, same station. I'll have a new investigation that has every chance of causing a stir, so I'm sure you're going to want to tune in: we'll be talking about the assassination of the young APM councilman, Paco Gómez, six months ago. You might remember he was found dead from a single bullet wound to the back of the head on the night of the elections in March. The crime remains unsolved, and his murderer is still on the loose."

Diego Martin's sign-off jolts her awake as she reaches to turn off the radio from where she has been dozing in bed. She never misses his show; it's her favorite, and she usually listens live, alone in the dark.

The journalist's parting words startled her. She gropes for the switch of her bedside lamp, then a cigarette, and with trembling hands tries to light it. Despite the late hour, she dials a number on her telephone. The line rings just twice before a surprised voice picks up.

"*¿Sí?*"

Even after living forty years outside of Spain, the woman on the other end still answers the phone as if she were living south of the Pyrenees. Never does she answer, "*Allô,*" as the French do. But it's less an affectation than a mark of resiliency.

"Did I wake you?"

"Not at all. You know very well I don't sleep much. What is it? Has anything happened?"

"No, not yet, but maybe."

She explains in a few minutes what she just heard on the radio. Silence on the other end of the line.

"Hello? Are you still there? Can you hear me? Well, what should I do now?"

"Finish your investigation and continue as planned over the next few days. Get some rest, too, and we'll just see what this journalist knows. I doubt it's much."

"OK, OK, but I can't help but wonder. He's an excellent investigative journalist, you know."

"It's normal to have a case of nerves, but don't worry too much, dear. I'm sure you'll pull this off. Everything is going to be just fine."

Soothed by the woman's reassurances and a hot herbal tea, she finally falls asleep. Starting tomorrow, she has a long road ahead of her. Her mission is only just beginning; she can't panic at every little snag. Even if shooting a gun is more difficult than she imagined. However, she has no other choice. A promise is a promise. She has to stay the course. For her. For her family. And for all of the others. Outside her window, in the sticky Madrid heat and in a few other large cities in Spain, there are people who have no idea she is aiming right at them.

2

A CHATTERING HORDE of Japanese tourists crosses La Plaza del Dos de Mayo, selfie sticks in one hand, shopping bags in the other, and crowd into the bar where Diego Martin is waiting for David Ponce for their monthly lunch date. It's a ritual they started a few years ago when the journalist and the judge were investigating a drug trafficking case, the tragic conclusion of which brought the two men close and marked the beginning of their friendship.

Ever since, they've met once a month in Diego's local watering hole, which is not far from his apartment in Malasaña, where *La Movida Madrileña** was born. More than a neighborhood, Malasaña is a symbol, but it is one that is struggling to hold onto its soul in the face of an increasing number of tourists and new arrivals. This once modest barrio was almost entirely abandoned before getting a second life when Madrid's artists and hipsters moved in. The tourist guides were quick to proclaim the news

---

*Cultural movement that began in Madrid after the death of Franco.

and, today, the barrio's pedestrian streets are lined with boutiques and filled with visitors from around the world, all while rents have exploded. The economic crisis that is rocking the rest of the country is unknown in Madrid's trendiest neighborhood, which retains the charm of an old Iberian village.

Nursing a beer, Diego checks his watch. As usual, the judge is running late. Diego fidgets with his pack of cigarettes and stares at the entrance, hoping to glimpse him through the crowd. It's an old habit he picked up working on a particularly sensitive investigation in Latin America. Never sit in a bar with your back to the entrance; always know who is coming in the door. He got that tip from some former members of the Pinochet opposition, and it has become his golden rule. It has already gotten him out of several jams in Mexico and Colombia.

Ponce finally walks in, exactly fifteen minutes late, which is to say on time for him. Even with a large shoulder bag slung across his chest, he tries unsuccessfully to push his six-foot frame toward the table at the back. The group of Japanese tourists is blocking his way, and Diego can sense his friend's growing frustration. Finally, his booming baritone and salt-and-pepper hair and beard cut a path through the crowd.

"Heads up, everyone! Coming through! You tourists, can't you see you're in everyone's way? Let's go, let's go! *Arigato*, yes, that's the way. Thank you, just move over there and stop taking pictures of everything."

Diego can't help laughing at the scene. He's still chuckling when Ponce flops onto the banquette.

"You can't resist, can you?" Diego teases him, in lieu of a greeting.

"Can't resist what?"

"Making a scene."

"Hold on, what was I supposed to do? Stand at the door for an hour? Besides, I'm starving. Let's eat first and talk after."

"Sounds good to me."

Tapas, of course; lots of tapas and two more beers. Planked cuttlefish, cider-cured chorizo, *patatas bravas, jamón y queso*. It's their usual menu, and they devour it in silence. Besides a shared aptitude for hunting down criminals, they have a common passion for food. They love to eat and eat well, which is to say rich food and lots of it. These monthly gastronomic lunches are sacred to them and merit their undivided attention. And their time. However long it takes for the bar to empty.

Stuffed, they order coffee and pull out their respective notes on their current investigation: the APM councilman who was assassinated the night of the elections. They shoot a look at the owner behind the bar, who gives them the all clear with a nod, and they take out their cigarettes. Only the regulars are left, and they won't protest; they know the owner's disdain for the public smoking ban works in their favor, too.

"Where should we start?" David asks.

"With the facts. I still can't understand how, in that exact place, at that exact moment, no one saw anything," Diego begins. "The cops have absolutely nothing? Not a single witness? Not a single clue? No leads?"

"Nada, zero. The investigation is at a standstill. Here, I made you a photocopy of the investigation file, which my incompetent colleague left sitting out on his desk. You can see for yourself: there's not exactly much in it. Except for the statements taken from his friends and family, it's empty."

"Friends and family, you say . . . Maybe that's where we should start looking?"

The victim, Paco Gómez, was from a good family, as they say. His murder, on the night of the elections and on a street so close to where the APM celebrated its victory, not to mention the fact that he was on course to become the youngest government minister in the history of Spain since Franco's death, made headlines for days afterward. But the investigation stalled, the new government began to make its first controversial decisions, and the front-page story was reduced to a few lines, all before disappearing completely from the media's radar. That is until today, because Diego has every intention of jump starting the investigation on his next radio show.

"What's your plan, then?" Ponce wants to know.

"I'll start by airing the interview with his mother. I'm meeting her tomorrow at her home. Then I'll do like I always do: I'll tease out some hypotheses. I asked Ana to give me a hand, find out if there isn't anything in his family life, any hints of drugs or sex. Give us something we can chew on. Speaking of Ana, there she is, punctual as ever, unlike some people I know."

Ana Durán and Diego Martin. Their friendship goes way back. They met fifteen years ago when Diego was working on a story about prostitution rings in Madrid. Ana was a hooker. The most sought-after transsexual working the Calle del Pez. The neighborhood diva. Blond hair, gray eyes, not tall but with impeccable plastic surgery. The doctor who operated on her in her native Buenos Aires did an excellent job; not a few of her johns had a surprise waiting for them. They all came back for more, though. So she stopped walking the street and began working from home, with the help of the Internet. In just a few months, she had become the top call girl at the biggest escort service. Charging two hundred euros an hour or a thousand euros for the night, she put away a small gold mine that allowed her to get out of the sex business and begin a new career: private detective. She opened her agency, Ana & Associates, on the same street where she'd worked, at home among the hookers and the trans. She is the sole employee, contrary to the name. Her little business is growing, however, so much, in fact, that she is seriously thinking of hiring some help.

"Ten years of walking the street empties your soul but fills up your wallet and your address book," she always says in the lilting Buenos Aires accent she still has, despite her long exile in Spain.

She's never short on clients. Sometimes they are the same ones who sought her out for her more "original" services back when she was working the streets. Her resolve and her determination quickly earned her an excellent reputation in her new line of work. It's not unusual for the police and even certain intelligence agents to consult her when their own leads go cold. Not always, but very often, Ana turns up either an answer or a clue to help advance their investigations. She has one of the best networks of informers in all of Madrid, hands down. Police officers, lawyers, judges, thugs, politicians, journalists; from Madrid's barrios to its government palaces, Ana knows them all. She's just as comfortable in a dive bar in the *gueto* as she is at an official reception at La Moncloa, the prime minister's residence, where she has been more than once.

Ana stops at the bar to say hello to the owner and order her usual *café del tiempo*, a very short shot of espresso that she pours over a glassful of ice, before joining her two compadres at the table.

"*¡Hola amigos!* What's new?"

"How do you drink that thing?" Diego's look of repulsion passes for a greeting. "Seriously, cold coffee like that, it's disgusting."

"You just don't know what's good," she shoots back teasingly. "So, aside from that, did you make any progress? Because I've got absolutely nothing. This guy led such a neat and tidy life it's almost irritating, at least for our purposes. He must have fucked twice in his life, to have his two kids. . . ."

"Shit, you didn't find anything?"

Diego is disappointed. He was counting on Ana to find some good dirt on Gómez.

"Nope, but you know me. I dug around anyways, and I've got a pretty substantial file for you. I concentrated on his family. Did you know that his grandfather and his father, who died last year, and his uncles were all Franco supporters?"

"His grandfather was labor minister, I think. I didn't know about the others. You think that's where we should be looking?"

"Hell if I know, but they were all in politics up to their eyeballs, usually in the shadows and always on the far right. The kid was following in the family tradition of course, but he chose a less hard-line path when he joined the APM in the 1990s. He was looking at a big career in politics if it wasn't for that bullet in the neck."

Same old, same old. The country voted an Amnesty Law—Diego calls it the Amnesia Law—shortly after Franco's death to avoid examining its troubled past. It's hardly surprising that the people who were protected by the law have simply adopted new tactics, them and their children and the children of their children. Democracy didn't really change anything. Worst of all, the new government is advocating a return to Franco-era values.

"What's your take on the murder?" Diego asks Ana. "It wasn't a bungled theft—he had everything on him when they found him: credit cards, money, and his phone."

"The cops aren't getting anywhere; they don't even have a hint of a lead—and even fewer suspects. It's starting to become an embarrassment for the commissioner," David adds.

"Damn it, how is this possible? We're missing something! Ana, keep looking, and let me know what you find. I'm going to put your file under a microscope. Who knows? Maybe I'll have a stroke of inspiration. . . . Mr. Magistrate, it's your turn to pay. *¡Hasta luego!*"

Her sandwich lies untouched on the table where she is sitting, on the patio of a bar in downtown Madrid. Her eyes are riveted on the black iron door of a historic, three-story building directly across the street. It houses offices, including those of the person she is there to see: Don Pedro De La Vega. *El Viejo,* as he is known in political and business circles, is as reliable as a Swiss watch. Monday through Friday, he keeps the same schedule down to the minute, takes the same streets, eats in the same restaurant, and leaves his car in the same parking lot. De La Vega knows something about parking lots: he owns a dozen of them throughout the city, and they earn him a tidy sum. Several million euros a year, actually. That's one of the interesting facts turned up by her meticulous investigation of her second target.

Ninety years old and one of the richest men in Spain, De La Vega continues to show up every day at his notarial practice. For the life of her, she can't understand why. He's got more than enough money to put his feet up somewhere nice on the Mediterranean—in Valencia, for example, his native city, which also happens to have everything you could possibly need or want to enjoy a lavish retirement. Instead, at eight-thirty on the dot every morning, he opens the office. Moreover, except for his lunch break, he almost never leaves it until ten at night. All the biggest players in business and politics, mostly those allied to the right of the right, have passed through his doors. If the rich live longer, bastards must have the longest life expectancy of anyone.

He's certainly in good shape: he still drives, lives on his own without a nurse or a bodyguard, and still likes to play a set or two every once in a while at Madrid's most exclusive tennis club.

It wasn't easy picking up the paper trail confirming El Viejo's vast fortune. Fake companies, secret bank accounts, tax havens, straw men, holding companies, subsidiaries, subsidiaries of subsidiaries. When it comes to hiding his net worth, this De La Vega is a regular pro. She had to spend a lot of time and call in a lot of favors from her contacts to track down just some of the assets of this former member of Franco's inner circle. Nevertheless, those that she found—even if they didn't amount to so much, she admits—were enough to earn him a place on her hit list.

De La Vega was one of Franco's legal advisors after El Caudillo came to power in 1939. It was a position he turned to his advantage, for himself and for his family, without appearing to break any laws, though his activities often crossed the line. But never ever did he get his hands dirty. Money and power exist to open doors and pay others to do the rest. Everyone has a price; the more you can pay, the surer you can be that everything will go exactly as you wish, no questions asked, no loose lips.

She has been watching De La Vega for several weeks, learning where he goes, what his routine is, and if he ever strays from it. Her conclusion—the irony is not lost on her—is that the best place to take him out is the underground lot where he parks his car every day. She staked it out carefully, driving in repeatedly, using different rental cars and disguises, parking in different spaces, and noting the placement of every security camera. She eventually decided where she would do the job: a poorly lit blind spot of a turn that even the ultra-sophisticated security system doesn't reach.

She checks her watch: 2:20. In ten minutes, El Viejo will enter the parking structure and get into his car to drive to his favorite restaurant for lunch. She gets up from the table, finishes her glass of water, picks up her things, and walks calmly to the parking lot entrance next door to his office. She is wearing a classically cut skirt suit and carries a designer handbag, a tote for her laptop, and a Bluetooth headset. She blends effortlessly into the crowd hurrying along the Gran Via. She could be any businesswoman in the sea of people on one of Madrid's busiest avenues. No one seeing her would ever suspect she was about to commit a murder.

At precisely 2:26, with her paid parking receipt in hand, she appears for all intents and purposes to be searching for her car. In fact, she is looking for a narrow service corridor she located on a previous visit, where she plans to wait for her future victim. She has five minutes to do what she has come for and exit the parking structure. She opens her handbag and removes a pistol and a silencer, which she purchased on eBay using an assumed identity. She takes a deep breath to calm her pounding heart.

It is now 2:29. One minute left. A car door shuts, and an engine starts. El Viejo is on time exactly. The large sedan approaches. Thirty seconds. She takes off her heels and steps into the middle of the turn. De La Vega arrives and throws on the breaks, surprised to see a barefooted woman gesturing at him to stop. He lowers the driver-side window.

"Are you alright, Miss? Is something wrong?"

"Are you Don Pedro De La Vega?"

"Yes, but how did you—?"

She pulls the trigger once, taking care to shield herself from any blood on impact. A single bullet enters the center of the forehead, almost at point-blank range. El Viejo's head lies on his seat, his eyes wide open as if he were thinking about something. A thin red trickle of blood is now running down his face. She puts her shoes back on and walks quickly to her car, barely a minute after having shot a man in the head for the second time in six months. At 2:32, she drives out of the parking structure. At the first red light, she opens the glove compartment, removes a piece of paper with several names on it, and, with a violently trembling hand, crosses out Don Pedro De La Vega. When the light turns green, she pulls out into Madrid traffic.

3

AFTER HIS LONG lunch break and meeting with his two closest friends, Diego walks back to Radio Uno, located in one of the tallest office towers in Madrid. The afternoon is mostly spent. In his bag are the investigation file that Ponce gave him on the young APM councilman's murder and the much thicker file that Ana put together. He crosses the building's cavernous lobby, nodding at the security guards, and gets in an elevator to the sixth floor. He rides it with several of his newest colleagues, all hired by Radio Uno's new director, who himself was named just days after the elections. The first move was to change the existing laws regulating public broadcasting, giving the government authority to appoint the directors of public radio and television stations. A move designed to muzzle the media from the get-go and send a strong, clear message: no opposition will be tolerated. Diego's new colleagues are clean-cut in all respects, and most are recent graduates of a journalism school in the north of the country. The school is run by Opus Dei.

The atmosphere in the elevator is frigid. No one says a word, and the icy silence is disturbed only by the noise of the elevator's motor. Diego amuses himself by staring fixedly at each of them in turn. None of them can hold his mocking gaze. They quickly avert their eyes or resort to pretending to look for messages on their phones. Whoever wants to climb the ladder of success at the station cannot risk the slightest contact with the in-house "Commie."

Diego delivers a well-aimed shoulder check to the person in front of him, opening a path to exit the elevator. He gets off and turns down a long hallway. Diego's tiny office—barely one hundred square feet with no air conditioning and a window no wider than an arrow slit—is at the end of it, sandwiched between a maintenance closet and the restrooms. Stuffed with files, books, and newspapers, it looks more like a storeroom than an office, and nothing in it conforms to current safety codes. It is the radio station's version of Siberia. There is a television mounted on one wall. A computer screen sits among the accumulated mess, but he has never turned it on; its keyboard is somewhere on the floor. Diego doesn't like computers, and he refuses to use the one supplied by an employer who is in the pocket of the new government. His own MacBook Air with a 4GB flash drive is enough for him.

In any case, Diego could give a damn about the size of his office. His top priorities are: investigating, getting out in the field, cultivating sources, and fact-checking. In other words, the ABC's of good journalism. A code of conduct that seems to have been forgotten for some time already. The only rule of the twenty-four-hour news cycle is to break a story, even if it means using unverified or even false information. Diego, on the other hand, likes to work at his own pace and take his time in adherence to "slow journalism," a protest against the mainstream media's churnalism and the cult of immediacy created by social media. Diego doesn't have a Facebook account and uses Twitter sporadically. He's also in favor of lifting confidentiality protections of legal investigations, which he considers a total hypocrisy with grave consequences. As if they were a guardrail that could keep his fellow journalists from crossing the limits of decency.

He doesn't keep any personal items in his office, with the exception of a black-and-white photo that he taped to the PC's permanently darkened screen: Carolina. His wife smiles at him in what appears to be a restaurant, her head tilted slightly to the left, her chin resting in her right hand, a usual pose for her, with her long, red hair falling on her shoulders and her bangs framing a pair of wide, green eyes. That was a long time ago, in a different life made for two, before everything fell apart one winter night. After ten years with Carolina, a phone call was all it took for the nightmare to start.

That fateful night, Diego was working late at home, reading the proofs of his latest book detailing an in-depth investigation he had conducted on Latino street gangs operating in Spain. A one-word text from one of his police sources managed to draw his gaze away from his reading: *estocada*. It was their code word for an urgent development. A system that served its purpose, saying, as succinctly as possible, that they had to meet immediately. The exact words used depended on the sensitivity of the information, but they always came from the jargon of bullfighting, which was their common passion.

Never had his informer given the signal quite this way. Diego understood immediately that something serious was going down. He dropped his papers and pen, shut off the stereo that was playing Pink Floyd, grabbed his jacket, cigarettes, and keys and went out without stopping to turn off the lights. He was only a few streets from their usual meeting place. On the way there, his phone was blowing up with calls: private numbers, friends, then the news agencies of the Interior Ministry and the Ministry of Justice. Something was up. He began to walk faster and finally started running. He had a bad feeling that was turning into a mounting panic. Despite the frigid temperature, he was sweating, his hands were clammy, and his head was pounding. In less than ten minutes, he was standing with his cop friend on the Plaza del Dos de Mayo, at the monument to Daoíz and Velarde, the two heroes of Madrid's popular uprising against Napoleon's army on May 2, 1808.

The cop, a member of the elite Special Operations unit of the Spanish police, was waiting for him at the monument's brick arch, and he looked like hell. Instead of shaking hands with Diego, he threw his arms around him.

"Diego, it's Carolina . . ."

"No!"

His cry tore through the Madrid night.

He sank to the ground before he realized what he had done. He was sitting on the cold concrete with his head in his hands, incapable of doing anything else. Numb. It took him several minutes to grasp what he had just heard. Then the questions came: "Where? When? How? Who? Why?"

"I'm really sorry, buddy. I don't know what to say . . . Come on, I'll take you to the coroner's office. You're in no condition to drive, but you have to identify the body. It's standard procedure," the cop said.

"That can wait," Diego shot back. His eyes were bloodshot, and he could barely stand up on his own. "First, I want to see where it happened. Do you know anything more?"

"Not yet. There's a unit on-site. If anyone knows, they do."

They drove to the Chueca neighborhood, where Carolina had been having dinner with friends, the same friends who had tried to reach Diego on his phone earlier that Thursday night in December. The restaurant entrance looked like a classic crime scene: yellow police tape, squad cars with their red lights flashing, gawkers. A white-suited forensics team was busy at work. They had already removed the body.

Diego had seen dozens of scenes just like it, in Spain and in plenty of countries in Latin America, enough to harden him against death and immunize him to the sight of corpses. But not that night. That night, it was Carolina. His wife. The woman he wanted to spend the rest of his life with. Whom he wanted to start a family with. They had made the decision only a few months before and had been trying to have a baby ever since.

It took everything Diego had to control himself when he saw the pool of blood where she had been gunned down. He saw David Ponce coming toward him and felt the judge grab hold of him as he started to fall. At that time, the two men were only professional acquaintances who held each other in mutual esteem and got along well.

"What the hell are you doing here?" Diego managed to ask.

"I'm on duty tonight. Listen, Diego, I'm so sorry. You know how much I liked your wife. The only thing I can tell you for now, even if it's not much comfort, is that she didn't suffer. She died immediately. I promise you, we'll do everything we can to arrest the people who did this."

"Tell me how it happened."

"Two guys were waiting on a motorcycle outside the restaurant. It all went down very quickly. The one who was driving started the engine, the one riding pulled out a gun, he shot five times, and they drove off. They were already long gone by the time the police arrived."

An execution, by the numbers. A modus operandi that was all too familiar to the police and intelligence services. The signature style of Latino drug traffickers. Despite the best efforts of Ponce and the officers assigned to the case, they were never able to close it. Carolina's murderer was never caught, and Diego hasn't been the same since. Her death was his fault; he would never be able to forgive himself. His investigations into the drug cartels had earned him many death threats. Several Mexican drug lords let it be known that he and his family would pay dearly if he stuck his nose in their business. Diego never believed a word of it. "There's nothing to worry about," he reassured Carolina. "The Mexicans aren't going to come all the way here just to shoot me." To assuage her fears, however, he cut back on his trips.

But drug traffickers stop at nothing to get revenge. With the help of his friend Ana Durán, Diego led his own investigation. And he discovered that the murder had been ordered by El Loco, the kingpin of the Juárez Cartel, one of the largest criminal organizations in Latin America. It was a Mexican federal narcotics agent who tipped him off. In typical fashion and true to his nickname, the drug lord told his henchmen he didn't want to kill the journalist so much as make him suffer for the rest of his life. So he ordered Carolina's execution. Diego and Ana also found out that the two hired guns flew in just for this mission. They arrived on a flight from Mexico at eight that night, killed Carolina at one o'clock in the morning, and were back on a flight and home again early the next day. The authorities had identified them but couldn't stop them in time. The driver later died in an AK-47 shoot-out between warring cartels. As for the gunman, no one ever found out what happened to him. Probably six feet underground, as well. In their line of work, life expectancy doesn't run high. Or that's what Diego hopes, at least.

After Carolina's death, he fell into a deep depression and has never really come out of it. He hardly goes out socially anymore and refuses any and all dinner invitations. As for meeting someone new, the idea has never crossed his mind. Five years later, his heart hasn't healed. Could it, someday?

Seated now behind his desk and pleased with the little provocation he directed at his new colleagues in the elevator, Diego opens Ana's file on the APM councilman, lights a cigarette, and starts to read the private detective's report. He has a nagging feeling that there is something different about this case, but he can't put his finger on it. It is just intuition. From force of habit, his hand reaches for the television. He turns it on but keeps the sound low. It's the news, promising a special report after the commercial break.

Isabel Ferrer spent the afternoon at home. The lawyer needed some time alone after a complicated morning and a tumultuous lunch. Thirty-eight years old, single, French, and with no children, this granddaughter of Spanish immigrants to France who carries passports of both countries has always felt an emotional attachment to her parents' and grandparents' homeland. After graduating magna cum laude from law school, the pretty brunette with dark eyes marched her five-foot-six-inch frame into one of the biggest criminal law firms in Paris. She worked her way up, case by case, client by client. From small-time dealers in the projects to the most dangerous felons to the most famous ones as well. Her early cases usually went immediately to trial, but her later ones were high-profile criminal court cases. She defended them all: con men, murderers, drug dealers, armed robbers, everyone except sexual predators. She refused categorically to use her skills defending rapists and pedophiles. It was the only part of her oath as a defense lawyer that she ever broke, the only breach in her personal code of conduct, based on the firm belief that every person, no matter the crime of which he stands accused, has the right to an attorney. But she drew the line at rapists: that was just too much for her. She couldn't say why, exactly, but that's just the way it was. And no one ever challenged her on it.

Isabel didn't win all of her cases—far from it—but her eloquence and her impassioned arguments could plant a seed of doubt in the minds of jurors and reduce sentences for her clients. Some in the media fell for her too, praising her as a symbol of a new generation of talented and attractive young lawyers: the beauties of the bar. Her success led to some memorable fights with her family, who never understood how she could defend a killer or a dangerous criminal.

At the peak of her career, at a time when she could have opened her own law practice, she ditched it all and took the opposite voyage that her father, mother, and grandparents had made. She crossed to the other side of the Pyrenees and settled in Madrid. All it took was a week: no more clients or cases, no more working for the Paris bar, and no explanations either. She dispatched her standing caseload, put her handsome apartment in

Neuilly-sur-Seine on the market (it sold in two days), got on a plane, and set her suitcases down in Salamanca, one of Madrid's most expensive neighborhoods.

No one understood, not even her parents. A sudden impulse that some of her friends and associates chalked up to burnout: the work was just too much for her. Others saw a gesture of grief, in reaction to the death of her grandfather, with whom she had been close; he had passed away only a few weeks earlier at the age of ninety-three. The only one who remained mute about her decision was the person who usually had something to say about everything: her grandmother. She held her granddaughter tightly in her arms at the airport the day Isabel left, but she never looked Isabel in the eyes, for fear it would make her cry. Isabel never looked back, passed quickly through the security checkpoint, and from there to her boarding gate. She was changing her life entirely, but, oddly, she felt calm, relieved even.

Today, however, she feels anything but calm. As soon as she got into her apartment, she took a shower. Even an hour under a powerful jet of hot water didn't relax her one bit. She tried to take a nap but couldn't drift off. She hasn't eaten since the day before and is having trouble concentrating because of a pounding headache. She puts two slices of bread in the toaster, and when they're ready, she pours a trickle of olive oil and a sprinkle of salt over them. Her grandmother used to make her the same snack when Isabel was a little girl. She forces herself to eat them with some aspirin to alleviate the coiling and uncoiling of pain in her head. Her day isn't over yet; she still has something very important to do. She has to look good, and, above all, she has to be on her game. She goes back to the bathroom to do her makeup, paying attention to the dark circles under her eyes and her tired complexion. From her closet, she selects a light-colored suit, and from the dining room table, she picks up a pile of papers and fits them into her purse. It's time. She is hoping that, at the Puerta del Sol, right in the heart of Madrid, a large crowd will be waiting for her.

A dozen or so journalists are already stationed in front of Calle de Cervantes. All of them are intrigued by the invitation they received from an organization they have never heard of, announcing a press conference and a big reveal: something of major importance, something big enough to shake up Spain's very democracy. At eight o'clock. Right on time to make the nightly news at nine. Luring the press was Isabel's idea: invite them, tell them, and let them spread the news to as many people as possible.

That's all it took for a pack of journalists to show up. TV station vans are double-parked in the street, blocking traffic. Crews from the national radio stations have parked their cars on the sidewalk. Two police officers are trying as best they can to keep order. One of them is requesting backup from headquarters, yelling into his walkie-talkie and gesturing so wildly that everyone walking past laughs.

Isabel has a hard time pushing her way through the crowd. When she gets to the door and the journalists realize she has the access code, microphones and cameras are swiftly pointed at her from all directions. They start to surround her, but she manages to get inside without having to answer any questions.

She joins her team on the second floor. There are a dozen people, mostly women, who have followed her instructions to set up the area for a press conference. There is a dais with a long table and some chairs, and on the wall are hung black-and-white photographs, along with a few in color, though yellowed with age. All of them are faces of children. Beyond the dais are fifty empty chairs; it won't be long before they are filled. There is no air conditioning; the air is almost too thick to breathe. The tension is almost palpable, too. What they are about to set in motion can't be stopped, and everyone there knows it. When this press conference is over, their lives will never be the same. They know there will be consequences. They're ready.

With her nerves on edge, Isabel greets the staff and then finds a seat without another word. She takes out her papers and looks them over. Then it's time. With a simple nod, she gives the signal. The doors open. In less than ten minutes, the room is completely full. While the cameramen set up their equipment at the back of the room and the radio reporters position their microphones, Isabel is imperturbable. She stares blankly ahead, oblivious to their questions.

When she senses the room is ready, she gets to her feet, and the crowd immediately falls silent. She hasn't said a single word yet. She gestures toward a door in the back, and five people, all women and wearing white masks, enter. They come forward hesitantly, warily, under the media's projectors, and take their seats with Isabel on the stage. Incomprehension plays across the faces of the journalists, who are wondering what all this can mean as they begin to text their editors: whatever this is, the pictures alone are going to go viral. Their frenetic typing on their smartphones ceases only when Isabel finally begins to speak.

"Good evening everyone. Thank you for answering our invitation. You are wondering undoubtedly who we are and why these masks. I want to reassure you: when you leave here tonight, you will understand why these women chose to remain anonymous for the moment. I am not one of them, but I am their spokesperson. My name is Isabel Ferrer. I am a lawyer, and I am representing these women and thirty other individuals, including some men, old people, and young people, who have decided to join together today to demand justice."

For a full twenty minutes, the audience seems to be holding its breath, hanging on Isabel's every word. She composed her speech as if it were an argument for the defense. The only difference is that she is standing not in front of a judge, jury, defendant, and plaintiff but before an audience of members of the press. She summons all of her energy, her strength, and her conviction. She knows she has the power to convince any listener and can find the right words, the ones that will hit home. Just like in a court. This is a case she intends to win in front of a judge and jury of journalists.

"I won't insult your intelligence by retelling the story of the dictatorship that began with Franco's rise to power. However, I ask you to remember that sinister period, to think back in your mind to 1939 and the dark years that followed. I want you also to remember his death in 1975, the transition period that began then, the referendum on the Constitution of 1978, and the Amnesty Law that was passed so that we could live today in a democracy."

Her speech sets off a flurry of quizzical looks, raised eyebrows, shoulder shrugs, and some impatient fidgeting in the audience. With the country again in the hands of the far right, her words hint at something worse to come for these journalists who are already battling restrictions on press freedom. Isabel falls silent for a long, strategic minute, an almost unbearable wait, before continuing to speak, with greater and greater confidence.

"I'm not telling you anything you don't already know when I say that numerous acts of violence were committed during the thirty-six years that Franco was in power. And that the transition to democracy could only happen because we have, all of us, chosen to close our eyes. Above all, the past had to remain undisturbed; the criminals could not be brought to justice. It's possible that what I am about to tell you will surprise you, but it is worse than anything you can imagine. I want to tell you about babies who were stolen and children who were forcibly taken from their "leftist" parents in an attempt to stomp out the opposition. I want to tell you about, not one or two kidnappings, but about a vast criminal organization created to take these children from their parents by any means."

Murmurs now, camera flashes again, pens flying across notebook pages, hands raised in the hope of questioning the lawyer directly. Nothing less than a government scandal is being brought to the public's attention. There were rumors, of course, and historians had found them plausible, but they were never able to prove anything. Isabel has entered her zone: she seems to take no notice of the commotion her words have caused. She continues to speak, oblivious to everything else, with the same assurance: the victims, she says, number in the thousands, even the tens of thousands.

"And the worst news of all is that this program survived after Franco. Believe me, for years following Franco's death, many 'good' Catholic families continued to 'buy'—there's no other word for it—these babies born into the lowest socioeconomic ranks of our society. This is why we are launching today the National Association of Stolen Babies, the NASB. We are a small group today, but we hope many more will join us in the coming days. We are calling, solemnly, on all those women and men who believe they were the victims of this trafficking. It doesn't matter if you are a child, a parent, or a family member. If you have the slightest doubt, don't wait. Come see us. We are not afraid, and we make this firm promise to those who knew and said nothing, and to those who are guilty of these crimes, that we will not let you rest easy. We will fight you to our very last breath. And to our government officials, we want them to know that we will not be stopped by the Amnesty Law. These are crimes against humanity, they are unconditional. The citizens of Argentina and Chile have done it. The time has perhaps come for us in this country, too, to search deeply in our past. And may those who should pay be made to clear their debts once and for all. We are tired of keeping silent. We can no longer ask these mothers and fathers whose children were taken from them to wait for answers any longer. Thank you for your attention."

Isabel stands, signaling that the press conference is over. There will be no time for questions, but she does let them know that more concrete details will be released in the coming days. Her strategy is simple: drop the bomb and let the media jump on it with their special editions, experts, and analysts of all kinds. Let them stew over it. Then return to the attack with micro-releases of evidence and historical documentation.

In the meantime, she needs to get some rest. She needs to get far away from the media hype that is going to build like a hurricane. She needs to spend time with the files she has put together, to learn everything she can from the first statements to come in from mothers and fathers looking for their children. She also needs to continue preparing for her next appointment. He doesn't know it yet, but there is a man out there who is about to cross paths with her.

4

DIEGO HASN'T SLEPT for days. The media storm that followed
the NASB's press conference upset everything in its path. No one
has been talking about anything else for the last forty-eight hours.
Newspapers, radio, television, Internet; no matter the media or
the time of day, in the street, in cafés, at work, everywhere. The
entire country is obsessed with the story of the stolen babies. As if
it had suddenly awoken from a deep sleep. Or a coma. For Diego,
that's the real story. But there's a problem: he wants his radio show
to continue as planned, only introducing this new story in incre-
mental doses. He knows that his listeners won't understand if he
just ignores it. But he also knows that running after the story is a
fool's game. Let the others have their conjectures; he will investigate but in his own time. That's his plan. It's easier said than
done, however, with a story as hot and as unavoidable as this one.

As soon as the association was launched, he began researching
it online and put Ana on the case. He didn't have to convince
her, as sometimes needed to happen in the past. The private
detective called him almost immediately to offer her services; her

Argentine blood was boiling. She was having flashbacks to when she was a teenager, which were her most terrifying years, when being gay, different, and wanting a sex change bought her prison time and torture. She eventually fled. Now the country that gave her a home is doing the same thing. The same system, the same ingredients, and the same victims. There are still kids in Argentina today who are searching for the truth. Others will be going through the same ordeal, here, in Spain. How many?

"It's insane, Diego!" she screams at him over the phone. "Do you realize? It's just like in my country, just like in all of these Latino dictatorships. Fuck, I can't believe it!"

"It's pretty incredible, all right. The main thing to find out is how many of them there are. I've heard rumors of several thousand."

"Can you imagine? Of course it's true. It's the same thing, only the names are different. What a bunch of fuckers! My god, to do that to kids . . . ? I'd just waste them. That's all they deserve!"

"Calm down, Ana. Calm down. OK, I know that's easy for me to say, and this is a subject that hits close to home for you, but you can't just say anything that comes into your head. Can I take it you want this story? Try to see what kind of initial elements you can find as quickly as possible. This story could bring down the government, not to mention the monarchy. It doesn't smell good at all. Look into this association, NASB, as well: Who's behind it? How many are in it? Who is financing it? Also, find out who this lawyer is . . . the one who gave the press conference."

"Oh, now that you mention it, I know her! Can you believe it?"

"What? You waited until now to tell me? Who is she? How do you know her?"

"She hired me a few weeks ago to put a file together on that Don Pedro De La Vega. You know, the filthy rich notary who was a big contributor to the APM."

"Why did she want it?"

"Beats me. You know I just do my job and don't ask questions. It was interesting, though. I'll tell you sometime. But what that means is that I have her cell phone number. I'll try to get in touch with her and set up an appointment as soon as possible. I'll keep you posted."

That's all they have time for. Diego still has to finish editing his interview with the mother of the murdered APM councilman, Paco Gómez. It's scheduled to air on his next show. Getting this exclusive interview was no small feat; he called so many times he could be charged with phone harassment.

It is the first interview the woman has given since the murder. To top it off, it is with a journalist who is not her cup of tea and whose ideology she doesn't share. She let Diego know it the minute he walked into her house.

"I don't like you, Diego Martin, and I don't like what you stand for. You gain audience ratings out of other people's deaths and the pain of families who have lost a loved one. However, I also have to concede that you are stubborn and persistent, which undoubtedly serves you well in your line of work. You don't let go of anything, which leads me to believe that if anyone can find out who killed my son, you will. And that is why I agreed to meet you."

It was a hell of an opener. Since his recorder was already running, Diego knew immediately he would play this introduction on the air. The rest was a typical interview, with just enough drama to grab listeners. Paco's mother is from that bourgeois milieu that abhors the expression of any emotion, especially in public. She fought back her tears until the last moment, answering in a quavering voice before finally sobbing uncontrollably at the final question. It's going to make for a great show.

Sitting in front of his computer with his headphones on and the editing program running, Diego struggles to concentrate on the task at hand. His mind is wandering, and he stares into space; he hasn't heard a single answer from his interviewee. Just then his phone rings, causing him to jump. It's a landline: David Ponce's. The judge almost never calls Diego from his office phone.

"David, how are you?"

"Fine, and you? Listen, I'm calling to confirm our appointment tomorrow night. It's at nine o'clock, correct?"

His friend's question and tone of voice are unusual, but Diego doesn't let his surprise show. Ponce has already shared with him his suspicions, namely that, as president of the left-leaning Association of Magistrates, his phone might be tapped. If Ponce is calling him like this, it's because he has something important to tell Diego.

"That's right. Nine o'clock. Let's meet in the café across from your office. I'm interested in hearing the Association's official position on this case," Diego adds.

It's a little lie, to let David know he got the message.

"Perfect! See you tomorrow night!"

After such a bizarre call, Diego decides to leave the editing for later. He has twenty-four hours until he meets David. It's enough time to keep digging into the mysterious stolen babies. However, there isn't much to be found online beyond the dozens and dozens of links to media sites around the world reporting on the creation of the NASB and the possible consequences these revelations could have for the country. In short, there is practically nothing at all. There are some anarchist blogs and comments posted on far-left discussion forums, spreading rumors about couples in the opposition who were murdered by Franco's police so they could steal their children and raise them Catholic and Francoist, or about abortions forced on women suspected of being part of the underground Communist party.

He's going to have to find some more reliable sources the old-fashioned way. He is going to have to go to the library and the national archives; he'll have to talk to historians and members of the opposition at the time, although their numbers are dwindling. Above all, he has to meet this lawyer for the NASB. She certainly knows much more than she let on in front of the cameras the other day.

Diego calls Ana. She picks up at the first ring as if she was waiting for his call and knew what he was going to ask. Before he can get a word out, she answers him.

"I can't reach her. She must have turned her phone off."

"Shit! Keep trying, call every ten minutes, but I absolutely have to meet her. She's the one with the information. She's the only one who can help us."

He's not optimistic though. It's going to take either a stroke of luck or a serious misunderstanding for her to agree to meet him. However, he's convinced she has at least some of the answers to his questions. Even better would be if she had concrete proof that would leave no doubt as to the veracity of her declaration. And that she would agree to show him. There's no harm in dreaming.

The train to Barcelona has just left the Atocha station. In two hours, she will be walking the famous La Rambla boulevard in that fabled city. She has an appointment with a doctor not far from there, on a tiny street in the Barrio Gótico. She has dyed her hair blond for the occasion. It brings out her wide, dark, almond-shaped eyes. It's best to take precautions when meeting this kind of individual. Wearing jeans, a T-shirt, and Converse sneakers, she looks like she's leaving on a long weekend. She doesn't plan to stay as long as that, however. As soon as the meeting is over, she will retrace her steps exactly. Depending on the time, she'll try to catch the last train, leaving at midnight sharp. In case she misses it, she has reserved a room in a small family-run bed and breakfast to spend one short night before returning to Madrid.

She shivers. The air-conditioning is on full blast. She is seated by herself in a window seat in a half-empty first-class car. Today's newspapers lie untouched on her tray. A small overnight bag sits at her feet. When the train conductor offered to place it in the overhead rack, she politely but firmly refused, explaining that it held her computer and that she was planning on catching up on work during the trip.

What it holds, mainly, is her P38 with a silencer. There is also a folder containing maps of Barcelona, some official documents, and a set of photos of a man that were taken in the street and a variety of public places with a telephoto lens: Juan Ramírez, the third. Named after his grandfather and father, of course also both named Juan Ramírez. All of them doctors and part of one of Barcelona's oldest families. Little Juan is married, a father of five children, and a practicing Catholic. He has one particular trait, however, for which his family has taken to calling him the "artist" of the clan. He plays the bandoneon, a kind of concertina typical of tango ensembles in Argentina. Every Thursday night, after his last appointment, Juan leaves his office in the chic and bustling Avenida Diagonal and heads for the Barrio Gótico, the Gothic Quarter. There, on the ground floor of one of its tiny, faded houses, he takes lessons from an elderly musician who came to Barcelona years ago from Mar del Plata and who is trying to inculcate in his student an appreciation for the spirit of this very specialized instrument.

Isabel knows all of this. She's been watching Ramírez for a while. She's the one who took the photos in the file and who gathered the documents on the Catalan bigwig and his family. It only took a few well-placed phone calls to some government agencies. It's crazy the amount of information that is out there and legally available to the public. You only have to ask for it. And, of course, to know whom to ask. Plus, if you're nice, they'll even email it to you the same day.

Ten days of close observation were enough for her to move in on her target and put together a plan. It was out of the question to approach Ramírez at his office or at home: too risky. On the other hand, it couldn't be easier to run into him alone after his music lesson. That plan would also buy her time to leave the neighborhood without attracting attention. With a little luck, in such a deserted street, there's even a chance that Ramírez's body won't be found for hours.

But she's not there yet, and fatigue has finally caught up with her, despite her nerves. The announcement of the train's imminent arrival at the Barcelona Sants station wakes her with a start. She lets out a long sigh and begins to gather her things. She glances at the newspapers she still hasn't read, picks one up at random, and turns it over to read the headlines. Not surprisingly, the front-page story is the NASB and its press conference the other day. A headshot of Isabel is crowned by the sensationalist headline: Isabel Ferrer: The Woman Who Wants to Overthrow the Monarchy. As if she could. Either they didn't understand a thing, she thinks, or they are really bound hand and foot by the government. It is surprising to see this from a supposedly left-leaning newspaper. But only if you don't know that its owner is in thick with the APM, playing golf and tennis with the most powerful ministers in the new government and making business deals with the party's bigwigs. Now that the major TV stations have been running her speech on a loop, she has become the subject of all kinds of speculation. Everyone wants to interview her, everyone wants an exclusive, and some have started investigating her background. She knows because her former boss in Paris emailed her to say he was being bombarded by phone calls from journalists in Spain wanting to know everything they can about her. He sent them packing, of course. To avoid any interruptions on this trip, she turned off her cell phone and left it behind in Madrid. She bought herself another phone with a prepaid card, just like the dealers she once defended. The only person who has this new number is her grandmother, whom she called as soon as she left the press conference. So as not to alarm any of her family and friends, she sent a group email to say that everything was fine but that she was going to have to cut off all communication for a few days, enough for the media hype to die down. She always knew her statement and the launch of the NASB would be a huge news story, but she never imagined it would be like this. Too much attention could be damaging to her mission.

She has three hours of time to kill before meeting Juan Ramírez face-to-face. She decides to take a walk on the beach at La Barceloneta, hoping the fresh air will clear her head. The wind gives her an appetite. She walks back into town and finds a table in a bar. She orders a local specialty: *pá amb tomàquet*, which is bread rubbed with tomato and olive oil. She's tempted to order a glass of wine but opts instead for sparkling water. She needs to have all her wits about her to kill the doctor.

Night falls at last. Isabel begins walking toward the Barrio Gótico. She wanders slowly through the neighborhood while checking her map, looking like just another tourist. Isabel is close to the street now. She slows down and then stops in her tracks when she sees Juan Ramírez, his bandoneon case in one hand. *Not yet. Stick to the plan. Wait for him to finish his lesson so that his teacher doesn't sound the alarm when he doesn't show up.* At least an hour to wait. She looks around: there's practically no one on the street. She can't stay here without attracting attention. She decides to retrace her steps to a busier section of the neighborhood. She finds a tree-lined square filled with teenagers practicing their favorite sport: getting drunk. *El botellón* is a game of street drinking passed down from generation to generation. The goal is to get plastered as quickly as possible. The pastime may be universal, but since Spaniards don't do anything like anyone else, they have a particular method all their own, which involves using a high-octane cocktail called *calimoxo*, a sickening mixture of Coca-Cola and wine. It does the trick though: two or three drinks in quick succession and you're guaranteed a hangover. Throw in a couple of firecrackers and it's a party. Isabel spots an empty park bench and takes it for herself. She watches with a pang of nostalgia as the kids show off. They remind her of the summer vacations she spent in Spain when she was their age when her parents would leave her with her grandparents, and she played the same drinking game with her cousins and their friends.

A car horn startles her out of her daydream. It's time. She walks, quickly now, to her third rendezvous with death. She glances to the right and to the left. No one is around. She is alone in the narrow, dimly lit street. Isabel takes out her pistol, attaches the silencer to the barrel, releases the safety, and then puts it back in her handbag, which she leaves open. She has already thought to tie back her long hair, so it doesn't get in the way. A door opens behind her: Ramírez. She turns around and walks slowly in his direction, looking to make sure his music teacher is back inside. One hundred feet. Her heart starts to pound. She takes a deep breath. Fifty feet. She reaches into her bag. Fifteen feet. He suspects nothing. She puts her hand on the grip of her P38. Six feet. Her breathing is becoming quicker and shallower. She draws her weapon at the same moment she comes alongside him, leaving him no time to react to what is about to happen to him. She pulls the trigger once. The gun makes a muffled grunt. Juan Ramírez falls to the sidewalk. Isabel does not even break her stride. She continues walking, unhurriedly. At the corner, she stops to turn around, wanting to make sure Ramírez is dead. The good doctor and bandoneon student lies motionless, face down, near the gutter and a trash can. Where he belongs. With the garbage.

It's too late to catch the train back to Madrid. The lawyer decides to spend the night at the bed-and-breakfast. Before Isabel gets there, she sends a text to her grandmother. A short message composed of a single number: 3.

5

IT'S TWO MINUTES past two in the morning. Diego leaves the studio, his usual cigarette hanging from his lips. This week's show, on the death of the APM councilman the night of the elections, was a hit. The audience numbers will confirm that tomorrow, Diego has no doubt about that. Radio Uno's phone lines were jammed with a record number of calls. The interview with the victim's mother worked its magic, no matter if Diego's investigation has gone cold. Even the best private detective in Madrid, Ana, hasn't found him anything. No witnesses. No clues. Just a man shot in the back of the head in the middle of the capital city. And no one who has claimed responsibility. It is bizarre. Truly bizarre. And it makes no sense, for the moment, at least. He's skeptical. Was Gómez murdered for financial gain? For political motives? Diego's going to have to keep searching. He won't stop until he gets some answers. In the meantime, he has other irons in the fire.

He knew going into the show that the current news cycle would play in his favor. Speaking live on a national radio station about an assassinated member of the ruling party, whose family was close to Franco, in the midst of a scandal ripping open old wounds in the collective memory of the country and the government, was sure to net a healthy catch of listeners. And it did. Hundreds called in, eager to talk about one thing only: the stolen babies. Among the callers there were the classic conspiracy theorist cranks accusing the National Association of Stolen Babies of being a left-wing cult and there were also die-hard supporters of the government, but there were also ordinary listeners who called to share stories they had heard in their families, or to recount episodes they had lived firsthand in those sinister days but that had taken on a whole new meaning for them in the light of recent revelations. Finally, more rarely, a few callers urged Diego to get to the bottom of the story as quickly as possible and to tell them if there was any truth to it. As always, he had to make choices. There were so many calls that Diego had to abandon his running order. No musical breaks or the book review. Only Prosecutor X was allowed to keep his three-minute spot to report on a case of sexual harassment implicating a Socialist city councilor. The show quickly became a debate stage. The story about the stolen babies is white hot, and a lot of people risk getting burned.

Alone in the hallway leading back to his office, Diego stops in front of the coffee machine, searches his pockets, locates some change, and slides the coins into the slot. The espresso is strong. And horrible. He'll dilute it with a finger of rum that he brought back from Venezuela and keeps in a drawer in his office. The bottle is a souvenir from a recent trip he made there to report on a rum plantation that hires only former gang members. They cut sugar cane in the morning and play rugby in the afternoon. The plantation is proving to be a clever way to keep them off the streets. For once, Diego had a feel-good story on the show.

Tonight, his thoughts are elsewhere. Still riding a post-show buzz, he's not ready to go home yet. After all, no one is waiting up for him there. And the story of the stolen babies keeps running around in his head. Diego pushes open his office door, turns on his desk lamp, gets settled in front of his Mac, plugs in an external DVD drive, and plays the recording of the show that just aired. Not to listen to himself—he's not such an egomaniac as that—but to make notes on the more significant stories that were part of the call-in section. Not the ones about stolen babies, per se, but about inexplicable events, strange meetings, and envelopes silently handed over. The stories were told with so many precise details that they could not have been made up. Diego's betting he might find something in all that. And if someone has some information that deserves a closer look, it will only be too easy to find them: everyone who calls into the show has to leave their phone number, and their identity has to check out.

He spends the rest of the night with his headphones on, scribbling notes. Finally, with his ears ringing and his mouth dry from the mix of too much coffee, rum, and nicotine, Diego decides to go home, take a shower, and sleep a few hours to give his brain a rest. His appointment with Ponce is tonight, and he's curious to find out why his friend asked to meet him near Ponce's office. Before leaving, Diego can't resist checking the latest news bulletins online. There is a breaking news flash, then another. From EFE, Spain's international news agency, and Agence France-Presse. The headlines are identical: terse, brief, and evidently a placeholder until more facts are known: PEDRO DE LA VEGA, RESPECTED NOTARY, MURDERED.

The subject of a future show, no doubt. Diego sighs deeply. There is also a message from Ana: the same news, and a request to return her file on De La Vega. Odd coincidence, he thinks to himself. But he's too tired to dwell on it. The sun is rising as Diego closes his office door. The beehive that is Radio Uno is starting to buzz. The morning journalists, who have been there since the middle of the night to prepare their shows, are going into the studio to broadcast on morning prime time. The midday teams are hurrying in, already stressed out, looking for any news they can put on the air as quickly as possible. An odor of cologne, warm croissants, and coffee suddenly grabs Diego by the throat. He feels sick to his stomach. He needs fresh air fast. It isn't until he is standing on the sidewalk in front of the station that he starts to feel better. A wave of fatigue washes over him. He hails a taxi. He could have taken the subway, as he always does in this city whose mass transit, chaotic at times, runs 24/7. But his legs feel as though they could go out from under him at any moment.

When he gets home, he doesn't even have the strength to take off his shoes. He collapses onto the couch and falls into a deep but agitated sleep. Ever since his wife died, Diego doesn't sleep well and suffers from sleep apnea, so much so that he never really feels rested in the morning. This explains the circles under his eyes and why he always looks half asleep, even in the middle of the day. The warmth of a sunbeam falling on his face, which sports a two-day beard, thick and black but speckled with gray, wakes him with a start in the middle of the afternoon. He feels as if he has cotton in his mouth, and his eyes are still blurry, but he grabs his phone. No response. Dead battery. When he plugs it in, it lights up with messages. Ana has called him a dozen times and sent him as many texts. She sounds amused at first, but her tone becomes more insistent with each new message, and she finally sounds pissed off that he hasn't returned her calls. She left her last missive only ten minutes ago. "Meet me at Casa Pepe. I'll be there in twenty minutes," he fires back without making any excuses for his silence.

When Diego rushes into Casa Pepe, their usual bar, his hair is still wet from a fast shower. Ana is sitting at the bar, and she doesn't look pleased to see him.

"Where the hell have you been, *coño*? I was starting to worry. I almost came looking for you at your apartment!"

"Well, you could have. You've got a set of keys. You would have found me crashed on the couch, snoring. I worked all night, and I was tired, OK? And my phone died. So you saw that your De La Vega got his head shot off. You think it's worth looking into, I suppose."

"That's an understatement," she answers him, rummaging through her purse and pulling out a thick folder. "Here, first of all, this is a copy of the file I gave to the lawyer. She seems to have fallen off the face of the earth, that one. No one has seen her since the press conference. But I'll find her. I'm not giving up hope. She'll have to turn up sooner or later."

"She's screwing around with us. Let's wait and see when she comes back from her vacation and with what news. In the meantime, what can you tell me about the notary?"

"Just read the file," Ana says with a note of agitation in her voice. "Take your time, but there's something that's bugging me. Someone I know at the morgue told me he died almost a week ago. But the family only made it known last night. I wonder why they kept the news to themselves for so long. I have a feeling they needed to put some order in the old man's affairs before going public with his murder."

"He was close to the APM—he must have had information on every member of the government, don't you think?" Diego asks.

"And on plenty of other people too, you have no idea. It's all in my report. You're going to freak out. We'll talk after you've read it. You're going to be able to do a nice show on this, just the way you like. A bit like last night's, if you see what I mean. You really nailed it, and it was great."

"Yeah, thanks," replies Diego. "I didn't do anything special other than hound the mother until she granted me an interview. The story didn't need any help from me. And then the callers had a field day with the stolen babies story. I have the impression we're going to hear a lot more about that. It's going to go on for months. Which is fine, because it gives us time to dig into it. I'm really pretty curious about it myself."

"You don't say. Well, I'm off," Ana says as she gets up to leave. "I have a job, you know, señor. I don't just talk into a microphone at night. I have clients who want answers to their questions."

"Oh sure, everyone knows about me: all I do is talk bullshit on the radio."

Laughing, they say goodbye, and Diego has two more coffees alone. It's still early, so he decides to walk to his appointment with David Ponce. Diego likes to wander the streets of the capital, avoiding the busy thoroughfares, strolling the narrow streets that are still unchanged by time, those that remain at least, moving at his own pace, his hands in his pockets, his mind working. He gets some of his best ideas while walking in the city like this. When they come, he writes them down in a little black Moleskine notebook he keeps in his jacket pocket, along with the Montblanc pen that Carolina gave him before they were married. He keeps it to remind himself of the past.

He still has time to kill, so he sits on the steps of the courthouse, which also houses the Audiencia Nacional, Spain's second highest court. Diego smokes a cigarette and plays a game with himself, imagining the lives of the people exiting and entering the symbolic building. Lawyers, judges, cops, defendants, witnesses, victims: theirs is a world where the worst is always happening, involving everyone from shady politicians and Basque terrorists to pedophiles, cheats, and wife beaters. After a little while, he walks into the café across the street, spots a quiet table in the back, takes out his Nagra and microphone, and orders a beer. He has felt the eyes of the other patrons on him since he walked in and has heard their incessant whispers since he pulled out his recording equipment. Everyone in this unofficial annex to the courthouse knows who Diego is. He's not exactly behind enemy lines, even if not everyone in the police and justice departments is his friend, but he rarely walks into the lion's den like this. David must have wanted them to be seen together, here, probably to give himself cover. But from what? Providing a journalist with his association's official position on the stolen babies scandal is a good pretext. Diego knows the judge well enough to guess that, somehow or another, David's going to pass him a message. What Diego doesn't know is whether it will be about this latest case or about a different one.

The two men exchange a firm handshake, polite smiles, and pleasantries. Their friendship is close but not well-known, and they can't show any familiarity. After a few minutes of small talk, just enough to take a few sips of their beers, they get started. Diego picks up his microphone and presses the record button.

"Judge Ponce, you are the president of the Association of Magistrates, your profession's second largest union. What is your position, as the representative of a Socialist-leaning organization, after the announced creation of the National Association of Stolen Babies?"

"As magistrates and professionals in the areas of law and justice, we're not entirely surprised. For some time, there have been rumors, some more reliable than others, about the trafficking of children. In addition, we know all about the crimes perpetrated by the Francoists during the Civil War and after, when they were in power. However, in this case, the accusations are so serious that we are asking in very official terms for an investigation to be opened. We understand and approve of this new association's request. The time has perhaps come for this country to finally examine this part of its recent history, as painful as it may be. The Amnesty Law, which was introduced at a time when the country needed to rebuild and close old wounds, cannot excuse every crime. We are also going to consult several elected officials on the left to gauge the likelihood of passing a bill proposing to abolish this iniquitous law and to put an end to forty years of impunity."

Simple, short, effective. It wasn't anything unexpected. David recited his official statement convincingly, as he does so well. Then, almost immediately, he left, citing work and an urgent case he needed to wrap up by the next day. As he stood up from the table, he took a packet of cigarettes and a lighter out of his jacket pocket, then shook Diego's hand and hurried out.

The journalist feels the piece of paper immediately. He makes a fist and sits back down, trying not to show his excitement. Impatiently, he finishes his beer and reaches his hand into his pocket to pull out some money while he drops the precious message in. It's not until he gets into the subway and satisfies himself that no one is following him that he reads it. A wide smile is still on his face as he taps the entrance code for his building.

The offices of the National Association of Stolen Babies are buzzing. The atmosphere is nearly riotous. Ever since Isabel's press conference, the phones haven't stopped ringing. The website, which went live the night of the announcement, has crashed several times: the object of a high volume of simultaneous hits, and also the target of an anonymous hack the previous night. The job had all the markings of the far right. On the home page, the association's introduction and menu were replaced by a huge black-and-white photo of Franco wearing, rather crudely, a slogan, or rather an insult, that leaves no doubt as to who ordered the hack: "*¡Viva Franco, cabrones!*" ("Long live Franco, you bastards!"). The NASB's volunteer IT team succeeded in taking down the message and the image, but they are still working on restoring the site's full content. They've been at it for hours.

The working conditions, however, are not ideal. The association's headquarters are small, much too small, and the computer programmers have been pushed to the back of the room where the press conference took place. There, they've had to make the best of it between tangles of cables, screens, power strips, and hard drives set up on two small tables and a few unsteady chairs that look as if they will buckle under the combined weight at any moment. Some programmers are seated on the ground, feverishly typing out hundreds of lines of code. One of them has been tasked with establishing some semblance of order so that no one makes the fatal error of walking on or tripping over a cord, which would shut everything down. Knowing such an eventuality could happen, they are wasting valuable time saving their work every ten minutes. The pandemonium is interrupted periodically by shouts of victory as team members restore a new page, a new sidebar, or a new article, incrementally bringing the NASB's website back to life. It was a cunning attack that forced them to rebuild the association's interface with the rest of the world from the ground up and to verify the security of its every nook and cranny.

A separate, smaller room barely holds another group of people. Their names are María, Ima, Daniel, Pablo, Josefa, and Elvira: the NASB's founding members. Some of them knew each other already, others met only a few weeks ago, if that. They have one thing in common: they are all looking for someone close to them, whether a child, a brother, or a cousin, who disappeared and was never seen or heard from again. They all believe their loved one to be alive, and each member is convinced that these people who have dropped completely out of sight are out there somewhere in Spain, living under different names, not knowing that their real families are looking for them or that they were the innocent victims of an inhumane, iniquitous system put in place by Franco and his henchmen. In age, they could be in their thirties or forties now; the oldest would be sixty-seven. That their numbers span several generations is proof that the Francoist machine was still working well after the death of El Caudillo. All the members knew they were exposing themselves by joining the association. They hoped that their lives would be changed by it. They knew it would be tough. But today, it's becoming too much. They are overwhelmed, by people just like themselves who are looking for answers, ordinary people to whom something truly unusual has happened. And by the media, too. Journalists are camped out on the doorstep of the NASB's headquarters, and they harass the volunteers for the one thing they want most: an interview with Isabel Ferrer. Some are even prepared to pay, and pay well, for the opportunity to scoop their colleagues. They are offering mind-boggling sums, large enough, some think, to put the association's finances in the black and finance a serious investigation that could uncover the truth. However, for the last three days, the lawyer has fallen off the radar. The situation is becoming worrisome at the same time the media is becoming more and more insistent, even aggressive. And so it goes in this kind of situation.

A veritable smear campaign has been launched against the NASB by a wide swath of Spain's media, from print and broadcast media to the Internet, all in the pocket of the APM. They are calling Isabel a traitor, a kook, a foreigner who has no business getting involved in things that don't concern her, a Communist (again), a Cuban or a Russian or a Chinese spy, whose mission is to destabilize the Spanish government. She has been spared no insult. The fact that Isabel hasn't responded to any of these attacks is only strengthening the arguments against her and shaking the resolve of the NASB's members, who are novices when it comes to dealing with the press.

A young blonde woman with sunglasses perched on her nose walks in. No one noticed her when she first came through the office doors. Without saying a word, she hangs her handbag carefully on the back of a chair, lays her laptop case on a table after making room for it by pushing aside a hard drive, and smiles at one of the computer programmers, who stares back at her quizzically. Then, she takes off her dark glasses and blond wig. Silence falls over the room. No one says a word. Everyone stares. The moment lasts only a few seconds, but it is as if time had stopped. She unpins a coil of her long black hair so that it falls to her shoulders then greets everyone with a timid "Hi," a smile, and a sigh. Before she has a chance to ask how things have been the last three days, the room erupts in applause. There are cries of joy and hugs. Everyone wants to get close to her, to welcome her back, or just say thanks or ask how she is. Surprised by their welcome, she stays in the room with them for several minutes, just long enough to get her head back in the game.

She finally manages to encourage her team in a voice loud enough for everyone to hear: "OK now, back to work! We've got a long fight ahead of us!"

As if by magic, the beehive starts buzzing again, and Isabel can take a deep breath. She needs to meet with the founders of the NASB. Find out how they are managing. Above all, share with them her strategy for going forward. She wants to hit hard, even harder than she did with the press conference. This time, she won't just be making accusations. She'll have proof, too. She won't give away everything she's got, of course. She'll keep some things secret for now. But the first documents to be made public are going to hurt. And hurt good.

Before she can cross the room to meet with the leadership team, a crowd begins to gather at the front door. Voices are raised;

a fight is brewing. Isabel comes closer. In the center of the circle is a tall, imposing woman who remains noticeably calm despite everyone else's agitation.

"I'll repeat: I just want to speak to Isabel Ferrer. And stop pushing me! I'm not a journalist, damn it! I know she's here, don't lie to me. So just go find her and tell her that—"

"It's fine, let her in. I'll take care of it," Isabel manages to say firmly enough to calm her staff.

As the others stare at them with both worry and confusion, the two women greet each other and then move to find an unoccupied table off to the side where they can talk without being overheard.

"Well, not to overstate things, it hasn't exactly been easy to reach you lately. . . . I left you twenty messages, at least," Ana begins. The private detective is smiling ear to ear, thrilled to be speaking to Isabel at last.

"What brings you here?"

"We have to talk."

6

OVERLOAD. JUST TOO much. Too many strange occurrences.
Too many deaths. Too many special editions. Too many bombs
exploding at once. Too many coincidences. Too many unan-
swered questions. Diego has worked on complicated investigations
in foreign countries. He's courted danger and been grazed by
death. He even lost the woman he loved. So he's not intimi-
dated by the stolen babies story. He knows what he has to do.
Remain impartial. Check every fact. Every statement. Every witness. Every document. For however long it takes to get to the
bottom of the story. No matter the consequences.

He could give a damn about consequences. It's only by working that he has been able to continue—or survive, rather—since
Carolina's death. If it weren't for *Radio Confidential*, he doesn't
know where he'd be now. After his wife's murder, he fell into a
deep depression and even contemplated ending it all. More than
once, he would have finished himself off with a bottle of pills, but
he could never go through with it. He was feeling better, until the
run-up to the elections. The new government doesn't know, and

will certainly never know it, but they undoubtedly saved his life when they kept his weekly two hours on the air. And now he's going to screw it all up with his investigation, guaranteed. He can see it coming, ever since he read the tiny piece of paper that David Ponce slipped into his hand at the end of their meeting. Just a few words, but it was enough for him to realize he's finally got something to chew on. Just the idea has given him back some of his hustle and the will to start over with a clean slate.

"I. Ferrer wants to see me in 48 h to show me files on stolen babies."

That's the message the judge passed him in the bar, and it's a ticking time bomb. The lawyer, Isabel, is clever, and she has obviously done her homework. She contacted the only magistrate with the cojones to help her. Nothing wrong with that, as far as Diego is concerned: since Ponce is his trusted source within the judiciary, Diego can bank on having a first-row seat to what happens next. He's going to have to proceed with caution, however. Diego can't risk causing Ponce any more damage than the judge might do to himself if he opens up an official investigation.

Which Ponce is entirely capable of doing, despite the pressure that will be mounting on him from all sides. If the government thinks it can sway him in any way, they are sadly mistaken. Way back when the Socialists were in power (Diego has to remind himself that the fascists were elected only nine months ago), Ponce sent them packing too, when he signed an international warrant for the arrest of Fidel Castro for drug trafficking, money laundering, and crimes against humanity. The ensuing diplomatic mayhem lasted for months. Cuba's cacique emerged unscathed, thanks to his poor health and his doctors' assurances—relying on what were most certainly fabricated lab tests and exams—that the harmless old man was senile, couldn't recall anything, and consequently could not be submitted to questioning. The proof? He stepped down and appointed none other than his brother, Raúl, to succeed him. Yeah right . . .

As soon as his mind was made up to make the stolen babies scandal his new priority—which is to say the second he read Ponce's note—Diego jumped into the hunt: for information, for witnesses, for evidence, and for time, too. He called the radio station to tell them he was sick and wouldn't be able to do his show this week. He talked it over with the programming director for a few minutes, and they decided to air a season best-of show in his two-hour slot. A sound editor was requisitioned for the task, and Diego has already sent him some clips that would work well. All of which buys him a few days during which he can immerse himself in the stolen babies story, starting now.

He's been at Madrid's main library now for hours. He was there when it opened, and he hasn't come up for air yet. He's reading history books, on the Civil War and on life under Franco, studies of government during the regime and political theory, too, and even some philosophy. He wants to have a clear picture of the context before going into the newspaper archives of the period. Diego was born in 1970; he was only a kid when El Caudillo died. He never really experienced the Franco era, or at least he can't remember it very well, so his first priority is this history lesson.

The problem with any kind of public building designed to serve the needs of researchers and students is that smoking is not allowed there. That means that if Diego wants to go out for a smoke, he has to turn in all of his books, and then when he has finished his cigarette break, he has to request them all over again. Whoever thought of that rule? It's now been four hours since Diego's last cigarette, and he's at his breaking point. He rationalizes that he can have a cigarette, stretch his legs, and clear his mind all at the same time. He can even check his emails and calls too because it goes without saying there is no Internet in the library, as if modern technology could ever disturb the years and years of dust that has accumulated on everything.

Out on the sidewalk, he looks for a bar. It's going to be lunchtime soon, but he can't find anything open at this hour. He sure could use a coffee, though. In this part of Madrid, as in many others in this city and other large areas throughout the country, it's getting harder and harder to find a place to sit and have a drink. The financial crisis wiped out everything. Some pockets of the city are utterly deserted. Entire residential communities too, which were developed willy-nilly by completely ruthless contractors and builders. Perhaps more than any other country in Europe, Spain has fallen on bad times and fallen hard. The country sank, literally. The same country that only a few years previously was cited as an economic model toppled like a house of cards. The politicians said it was globalization, and piss off. The real reason was an economy that doesn't produce anything anymore and a housing bubble. Buy, buy, buy was their cry to anyone who would listen, and there were many who, after forty-five years of dictatorship and shortages, ran as if for their lives to the banks and the builders. It was those same banks and builders who knew a good deal when they saw one and didn't hesitate to play the opportunity to their advantage. They gave out credit like chorizos. Twenty-, thirty-, forty-, even fifty-year mortgages. Come on, you need money? No problem, take it! Just spend the rest of your life paying us back. And if you can't, don't worry—your children will assume your debt for you. End of story: when the bubble collapsed, and when the foreclosures started, those proud Iberian property owners had no choice but to go live with their parents. When you're already forty or fifty, that's tough. Because if being kicked out of your home wasn't bad enough, a lot of the same people lost their jobs too. Factories shut. Small businesses closed. People with graduate degrees were willing to take any little job for whatever it paid, and millions of unemployed workers are still waiting in line, day after day, at job centers, at welfare, at aid associations, and at soup kitchens too. No roof over their heads and no job either. What a beautiful country, this Spain that played host to the Olympics, this young, modern democracy that rose so high and so quickly. There are some who might take offense at this, but most people are standing in such deep shit that they don't even realize that someone is responsible for what happened to them. All they can think about is whether they are going to eat, not at the end of the month, not at the end of the week, but today. In other words, it is a return to the past, to being a third-world country. And yet they still voted massively for the APM instead of taking to the streets to smash the whole system to smithereens.

Diego's mind races while he searches for somewhere to get his hit of caffeine. After ten minutes of wandering the neighborhood and cursing to himself, he spots a green-and-white sign. He's going to have to make do with a cardboard cup of coffee-flavored water at Starbucks and pay over five euros for it to boot. Well, it's better than nothing. He takes his first gulp and then decides to look at his phone. He scrolls through his inbox, sending most of his new emails to the trash (invitations to parties sponsored by all kinds of brands of liquor and telephone companies, press releases for the latest must-read work of fiction, and, of course, spam announcing that he has won a million dollars in Gabon's lottery). More importantly, there is an email from Ana. That one he reads immediately. Finally, some good news. The detective has managed to speak to Isabel Ferrer. The lawyer is willing to grant Diego an exclusive interview, but on one condition: that he dedicates an entire show to the stolen babies. She will even help him by putting him in contact with someone, whose name she wouldn't divulge, who will tell him a story that, and she insisted on this point, he is sure to find both moving and chilling. Isabel also wants time to answer the accusations made against her, so she can defend herself and explain why she has taken up this cause. She promises not to grant any other interviews to any other journalist: Diego will be the only one to get this scoop because she has great respect for his work. She agrees to meet him but not for another day or two because, as he might suspect, she has too much to do at the moment.

Diego tosses the rest of his coffee in the trash and walks quickly back to the library. He has a lot to read and less time than he thought to process it all. If the lawyer keeps her promise, and he has no reason to suspect Isabel won't, Diego's going to have to pick up the pace. It's an opportunity he can't refuse. So what if it messes up his timing a little? He's thinking already about the trailer for his exclusive report. And the audience numbers it will rake in. It's going to be a huge success for Diego, and for Radio Uno, which, despite being a public radio station run by directors who are little inclined to bite the hand that feeds them—the APM's cabinet secretaries and elected officials—would never dream of taking a pass on this story. He's going to have to wait to find out when the lawyer can meet him, though. And what she's got to show him.

The questions came fast and furious after Isabel finished talking to Ana. The NASB's executive committee was on pins and needles to find out who this woman was, what she wanted, and what Isabel told her. The lawyer was reassuring in her responses: the woman is a private detective whom Isabel knows and trusts and who could prove extremely helpful to them in the coming weeks.

What Ana didn't tell Diego in her email was that she offered Isabel her services, at no charge, of course. Ana's way of joining the fight. The association's spokesperson knows Ana to be extremely serious and effective at her job. The report she wrote on De La Vega was impressive in its precision, its scope, and its detail, gleaned God knows how. She didn't realize it when she hired the detective for that delicate job, but in Ana Durán, Isabel has found a solid ally. And she plans to put Ana to good use.

The icing on the cake, and something else Isabel didn't know, is that Ana is a close friend of Diego Martin. And so Ana passed him the message. After thinking it over for a long while, Isabel persuaded herself to go ahead, on the grounds that there was really no other journalist she could go to with her story. What's more, by getting close to him, she might be able to find out what he knows about the murder of the APM councilman on the night of the elections. The show he aired the other night on that topic didn't offer any new information, except for the interview with the mother, but Isabel is worried nonetheless. The smart thing to do is to get the journalist on her side. If she has to choose one for that purpose, she's certain it should be him.

The day is almost over. Isabel hasn't left the NASB's headquarters since she arrived that morning. There had been too much to do: communicating with the staff, explaining to the volunteers what she expected from them, putting into place a plan for more efficiently treating the requests that keep flowing in from potential victims, prioritizing the calls and emails that are piling up, meeting with everyone in the office, teaching the staff how to field questions from the press, and putting the final touches on a statement they are to use from now on and follow to the letter. Finally, she was able to spend some time on the task for which she accepted this job in the first place: studying the first serious cases of stolen babies that the association has received. That involves reading the documents, sorting them, and checking out their stories. All that in the office's highly charged atmosphere. She's going to have to consider finding a bigger office, and quickly.

The night has brought a welcome calm: fewer people, and less noise. Also, a palpable fatigue. Most of the volunteers have gone home, hopeful, but doubtful too. Exhausted, Isabel decides to head home as well. She sticks her head out of her office to let the two computer programmers know she is leaving. They are still glued to their screens, but they made huge progress today: the NASB's website is up again and fully operational, or almost. There are still a few wrinkles to iron out, but the site is running smoothly. The question now is, for how long? The hackers working for the far right will certainly attack again before too long. But there are firewalls now that, hopefully, will do their job next time. Before leaving, Isabel ties up her hair and puts her blonde wig back on. Even though it is late and she plans to exit through the building's basement, she prefers to take every precaution possible to avoid not only the press but also the cops and the Interior Ministry's surveillance teams, who will undoubtedly be staked out in front. In her situation, a little paranoia can't hurt.

Isabel refused to follow the advice of the association's cofounders to hire a bodyguard. No, she told herself: she has always lived alone, has always managed alone, and has no intention of changing. In any case, she can hardly allow herself to be herded around if she hopes to carry out her mission. Both her independence and discretion are the keys to the NASB's success, and there is no margin of error in her plan. So when her picture was published on the front page of all the papers, Isabel felt exposed. She had anticipated something of the sort, and she had bought what she would need to disguise herself. She put it all carefully away in her bedroom closet, which now looks like a theater dressing room.

Only a few minutes after Isabel's departure, one of the two computer programmers still in the office decides to follow her lead. Hours of coding have worn him out. That leaves only one person left in the NASB's headquarters, and it will be up to him to lock up and set the alarm on his way out. But he's not ready to leave yet. There are still a few things he wants to wrap up, and he has an important call to make. He waits a minute to make sure he is alone, then he begins to walk through the office, riffling through papers lying about and even taking photos of a few of them. Then he sits at Isabel's desk and turns her computer on. No security code. No password. He grins, marveling at what amateurs these sorry people are. He inserts a flash drive and saves onto it a copy of the list of names and addresses of everyone who has contacted the NASB since its launch. The process takes only a few seconds. After double-checking that he is leaving everything as he found it, he turns off the laptop and the lights and leaves the premises.

He is barely out the door when the person he has just phoned picks up.

"It's done," he says.

On the other end of the line, a deep, almost cavernous voice answers him.

"Good. Continue to follow instructions. You have an appointment in exactly thirty minutes. Go there directly."

"Yes, Father."

At home now, Isabel's day isn't over yet. She knows she still has something important to do. And it's not something to be taken lightly. Before getting started, she pours herself a glass of Rioja and removes from the fridge some sliced *bellota* (the best serrano ham there is, a small luxury that she allows herself from time to time) and a whole camembert. Purists would be scandalized by her combination of this ham, a treasure of Spain's gastronomic heritage, with cheese—moreover, a French cheese. But some people will never change. Isabel may be Spanish, but she is no less French. The advantage of holding two nationalities is that you can have the best of both worlds. She gets comfortable on the couch with her dinner tray and turns on the television. After zapping frenetically through the channels, she stops at a rerun of a crime telenovela, *Sin tetas no hay paraíso* (*No tits, no paradise*). She had heard of this soap opera about Colombian drug traffickers when she was living in France; the title made her laugh out loud at the time. She eats her dinner slowly to savor it and finishes her glass of wine, then gets up to fish a thick blue folder out of a chest of drawers in the dining room. It is bursting at the seams and marked with a white label on which she has written in black marker a single number: 4.

She opens it and begins to look through pages she printed out from different Internet sites, having carefully laid out on the coffee table a series of photos of a man in a business suit. If she wants to pull off their meeting tomorrow, she needs to check some details, go back over a few documents, and, most importantly, clean her weapon.

7

A LARGE MANILA envelope was sitting in front of Diego's apartment door this morning. He almost tripped over it as he was leaving. No name, no address, and, obviously, no return address either. As a journalist, he is used to receiving compromising documents on this or that public or political figure; sometimes they are copies of police statements or anonymous letters accusing someone known to the sender of the most heinous acts and threats. Until now, however, Diego has only ever been sent these at work, never at home. Who in the world could have left these documents at his front door? Who has his address, and who could even get inside his building? He's asking himself these questions as he walks toward the exit and begins breaking the seal. He sticks his hand in and cuts his thumb on a paper clip that is holding a handwritten note:

> *When you have finished reading these pages, the only thing left for you to do is get on a flight to Paris. My source is waiting for you there. She is ready to tell you everything.*

It is signed *Isabel Ferrer.*

Reading the signature almost knocks the breath out of him. He turns back immediately. He has to see what's in the envelope, right now. He clears away books, dishes, newspapers, glasses, and beer cans to make room on his dining room table. Cleaning and tidying were never his strong suits, and he has made even less of an effort these last few days. With a cup of strong coffee in one hand, he turns on his computer and pulls out the file the lawyer has left for him. He doesn't know why, but he's positive that it was Isabel Ferrer in person who came right to his front door.

Diego can see almost immediately that he is holding indisputable evidence that at least one baby was taken by members of Franco's regime from parents who were in the political opposition. If the association's spokesperson can find others—and it will take a lot of others—she might be able to prove her accusation of a scandal, but the reach will depend on the number of children removed forcibly from their parents. A birth certificate dating back to the Franco era on which only a first name was recorded. A certificate of death dated the same day. Also, several notarial documents pertaining to the adoption of a little boy (the name was carefully crossed out) who was legally abandoned by his mother—apparently because she was too young to raise him. The other documents are in the same vein. All are photocopies, but Diego is sure that Isabel Ferrer has the originals locked up tight somewhere. In a smaller envelope, he finds a plane ticket for Paris and a note indicating an appointment with an address and a time. The flight leaves early the next morning: Vueling's first plane of the day out of Madrid–Barajas Airport, leaving at 6:40 a.m. The return is for the same day, on the last flight and arriving in Madrid at 11:55 p.m. All of a sudden, tomorrow is stacking up to be quite a day.

That only leaves him a few hours to get ready. As soon as he gets to his office, he checks that his recording equipment is working, puts more than one battery in the charger, just in case, and makes two copies of the file found on his doorstep. He plans to glean everything he can from it and from his meeting in Paris for his next show, even though he still can't guess what he's going to find out there. The envelope didn't mention a name, only an address. However, the fact that the lawyer spent almost her whole life in Paris leads him to believe he is going to meet a key source in the French capital. Diego spends the rest of the day in his office, leaving for only a few minutes to grab a sandwich. During his break, he calls Ana to fill her in. She can't help but laugh at Isabel Ferrer's audacity and admire her for it too. They agree to meet at the end of the day so Diego can give Ana one of the copies he made of the file. One can never be too cautious under the circumstances. With documents as compromising as these, it will be safer if he shares them with a few trusted collaborators. For now, he still has to write up the running order sheet for Friday's show and send it to both the producer and the on-air director. He has no intention, however, of giving them a heads-up as to what he has planned, so he makes a fake sheet outlining a phony but plausible show, part of which he might have aired if a file of papers and a trip to Paris hadn't thrown a wrench into the works. He'll keep the real show under wraps until the last possible moment; in other words, two minutes before airtime, just as he gets to the studio. It will be too late for his producer to put the brakes on the show, which promises to set off yet more fireworks. Radio Uno's executives won't be very amused. As usual. And, also as usual, Diego couldn't give a damn.

Trembling with impatience, Ana is standing at the bar with a half-drunk Coke Zero when Diego arrives at Casa Pepe. Before he even has a chance to sit on the stool next to her, she starts bombarding him with questions about the contents of the documents.

"Look, just read them and see for yourself," Diego teases her in reply, not without a smile.

"Stop it! Tell me! Is there at least any proof of any kind of trafficking of children?"

"Looks like it to me. But there's something, in particular, that might interest you. . . . A notarial certificate signed by someone you know."

"What? Who?"

"You can't guess? Didn't Isabel Ferrer ask you to investigate De La Vega? It can't be pure coincidence. He played a key role in the adoption of a little boy in 1946, signing all the paperwork. It's not implausible to conclude he was part of the whole system."

"I remember seeing something like that when I was investigating him," Ana replies. "But I didn't think too much about it. I just thought it was part of his job. But, hold on . . . Could that have something to do with his murder?"

"No clue. As far as I can tell, it's too early to jump to conclusions. The old man certainly had a lot of friends in high places, but he had just as many enemies, too, who could be capable of anything. Let's say it's one of any number of hypotheses that could be worth checking out."

He orders a beer and grills Ana on her meeting with Isabel Ferrer. The private detective tells Diego how she waited for hours in front of the NASB's headquarters until she finally saw its spokesperson arrive, then sums up their brief discussion. Ana also explains to Diego how she had to offer her services to the association.

"Well, I should have expected that," Diego tells her. "You're right to do it. And they're going to need an investigator with your talents. But try to remain discrete all the same. I wouldn't want something to happen to you. If this lawyer is right, this could go down very badly. And you know as well as I do that the government won't hesitate to use any means necessary, legal or illegal, to protect itself. They did it with the ETA; they can do it again."

"Don't worry. I know what I'm doing," says Ana. "I'll remind you that I escaped without a scratch from under the boot of the Argentine generals. Well, almost without a scratch. In any case, someone's got to do it, and it may as well be me. And that way, I'll be the first to find out anything, and I can pass it straight to you. But listen, you've got a plane to catch at the crack of dawn tomorrow. Try not to miss it, will you? Don't stay up all night."

"Yes, Mommy!"

Diego walks home feeling reassured on the one hand and worried on the other. With Ana working for the NASB and in close contact with Isabel Ferrer, he can be sure he will be the first and the best-informed journalist in all of Madrid. He wonders, though, if his friend isn't putting herself in harm's way. He knows only too well where that can lead.

She made the right choice to rent a full-size sedan. At the very least, it's comfortable: leather interior, tinted windows, and deep, wide seats. She can even stretch out her legs. On the passenger seat, she has spread out a couple of files. On the dashboard, she has placed the envelope labeled "4." She won't need to look at that again. By now, she has memorized its contents by heart. And she knows exactly what her target looks like. After leaving Madrid, Isabel drove for thirty minutes until she got to the ultra-chic Moraleja district, located ten miles or so from the city center. She drove twice along its perimeter, then several times past a large, white villa with red shutters that had a high wrought-iron fence and a thick hedge protecting the house from prying eyes. She finally parked on the edge of the forest that circles this affluent enclave and that is home to Spain's wealthiest and most famous personalities.

One of these is Adolfo Ibañez. The president and CEO of the Mediterranean Savings Bank was born and raised here. Adolfo's father founded and built the bank and was one of Franco's financiers. His father also played an indispensable role in a number of financial transactions, some of which allowed certain groups on the far right, such as the Phalanx, to line their coffers. He ruled over his bank with an iron fist right up until he died, which was an eventuality he had prudently anticipated by handing the reins off to his son. For the last ten years, Adolfo has run the bank that made its fortune in the Franco era, and then he dropped off the radar before returning to prominence in the wake of the APM's election victory. Easy enough to do when certain cabinet ministers draw fees from the bank by serving on its board of directors. Twenty-five thousand euros for a place at the table, a perfectly legal guarantee of currying favor in the halls of power. It was also a form of insurance against the possibility that any legislation that would force banks to prevent money laundering or to report on the financing of political parties could tarnish its reputation and put a damper on its booming business.

Isabel wasn't surprised to discover a link between the APM and Mediterranean Savings Bank. To tell the truth, it doesn't even interest her. What does interest her is whether Adolfo Ibañez is going jogging today. Whether he will leave his house, take a left, continue on into the forest, run around the lake, and follow the same route to return home. It is an hour-long jog that he takes three or four times a week, early in the morning or late in the evening, depending on his work. She bet that he would get a workout in the morning today. So she drove out in the middle of the night. Since 3:00 a.m., she has been waiting for him, comfortable in her luxury rental car, which she has parked discreetly at the head of a small trail. The banker should run very close to where she is. But he won't see her.

It's still dark outside. A baroque ensemble is playing softly through the car's speakers: the final notes of Mozart's *Requiem*, sung by the exceptional voices of the Montserrat Boys Choir. Isabel likes to let her thoughts drift away on a piece of classical music. It calms her. Makes her feel better. She set her phone alarm in case she dozes off, which is exactly what happens. Her iPhone's beeping pulls her out of a light sleep. It's five o'clock, and the forest is waking up, but the residents of Moraleja are still in bed. She rubs her eyes and wipes a damp towel across her face, takes a thermos from a plastic bag, and pours herself a cup of hot coffee. She even risks getting out of the car to stretch her legs and answer the call of nature. She's been holding it in for hours and can't wait any longer. Anyways, she'll have a better chance of hitting her target if she doesn't have to pee. The only observer of her quick escapade is a passing deer. No reason for alarm: the animal is unlikely to go to the cops to report seeing a woman crouching in the bushes just before Adolfo Ibañez died.

Before getting back in the car, Isabel opens one of the rear doors and pulls out a long black case. She removes a rifle and places a telescopic sight on it and a silencer on its barrel. She takes five bullets and loads them into the magazine. She's feeling very sure of herself, but she prefers to have enough ammunition for any eventuality. It is the first time she will take aim from such a long distance. Even with the sight, she tells herself that she might have to shoot more than once to hit him. Especially since her target will be moving.

The sky is starting to lighten. It will be sunrise any minute. Isabel takes her seat in the car and lays the rifle down next to her. Her plan is to let the banker run by once before setting herself up for his return approximately thirty minutes later. That's when she'll have to leave the comfortable interior. She'll take position outside behind the engine, which she'll use to steady herself and hide partially from view. At exactly 6:12 a.m., Adolfo Ibañez runs quickly past Isabel at a distance of about one hundred and fifty feet. He suspects nothing. Only minutes away now. Isabel lights a cigarette, smokes about half of it, takes a few sips of water, then decides to pick up the rifle. She lays a blanket near the front right tire so as not to get herself wet in the morning dew. She waits. At 6:47 a.m., she spies in the distance the silhouette she has been waiting for: her target. He is coming, headphones on, his face redder than it was before. Isabel picks up the rifle, kneels down, steadies herself against the car, and looks through the sight. Adolfo Ibañez appears, as if he were a character in a video game. Almost unreal. Isabel inhales deeply, holds her breath, aims at his forehead, and pulls the trigger. Less than a second later, the banker is lying on his back on the ground, blood running from a hole between his eyes.

The lawyer doesn't move for a full minute. Then, without even approaching the body to look for signs of life, she disassembles the rifle, picks up the shell that dropped at her feet, tidies up inside the car, and then puts the key unhurriedly into the ignition. It is not yet seven in the morning. She doesn't want to take too long to get back to Madrid. The morning rush hour will start around eight o'clock. As she merges onto the highway leading into the city, she can't help but smile. It only took her a single shot. If her shooting instructor could see her now . . . Isabel thinks about the hours she spent at the police shooting range in Paris, located underneath a parking lot off a busy avenue near the Champs-Élysées. Call it a professional perk for criminal lawyers. Not many civilians are let in on the Paris cops' best-kept secret. A rare exception can be made, however, for people they like, such as Isabel. She's still feeling a little nostalgic as she closes the door of her apartment behind her, exhausted from her mostly sleepless night. She never even noticed the delivery van parked in front of her building.

8

DIEGO FEELS A hand on his shoulder and jumps. It is only the smiling flight attendant asking him to turn off his iPhone in preparation for landing. He does as he is told and takes off his headphones. He was listening to a live album by Noir Désir, a French rock band he discovered a few years ago but that he hasn't listened to for a long time. As he was settling into his seat to catch up on lost sleep, the thought of waking up in Paris gave him the idea to try them again. It couldn't hurt his French, either. He had been troubled by the story of this band and its lead singer, who went to prison for beating his girlfriend to death. He had even discussed the case on his show.

He stretches as best he can, rubs his eyes, and looks out the window. The sky is overcast, but he can make out the outlines of Paris through the clouds. He can see the top of the Eiffel Tower and the Stade de France, where he was never so cold as that January day when France played Spain in the stadium's opening match (who schedules an outdoor match in winter?). The Airbus continues its descent, and the Sacré-Cœur Basilica appears. In less than an hour, that's where he'll be, he tells himself. His appointment with an undivulged source as set up by Isabel Ferrer will take place precisely there, in the 18th arrondissement.

"Welcome to Charles de Gaulle Airport. The ground temperature is sixty degrees Fahrenheit; the skies are cloudy." The wheels have only just touched down, but already the air is filled with the clicks and beeps of seat belts unbuckling and emails and texts arriving. Diego doesn't move a muscle and watches with a mix of exasperation and scorn as his fellow passengers spring into action. He has never understood this frenetic need to deplane before the cabin door has opened. Hurry, hurry, time to leave. Quick, quick, be the first out the door. Faster now, make sure everyone appreciates what a rush you are in. He waits until the cabin is almost empty, then he stands, grabs his bag, and thanks the flight crew on his way out. His first priority is to get outside where he can smoke a cigarette, send Ana a message that he is "in the zone" (a little ritual of theirs), and find the commuter train into Paris. He wouldn't dream of taking a taxi. Too expensive. And what's worse, if his memory serves him well, the drivers are just too stupid, as tourists from around the world can attest. Diego wasn't favorably impressed by his last ride in a Paris taxi: it cost him over fifty euros to drive two miles from the Porte Maillot to the Porte d'Auteuil. When he finally met up with his friends, they assured him he had definitely been taken for a ride.

After some trouble figuring out the automated ticket machine, he manages to pay his fare and board the train heading into Paris. Forty-five minutes later, he is standing at the top of the

Lamarck–Caulaincourt staircase, in the heart of the Montmartre district. Diego's early, so he crosses the street to the café on the corner. He hasn't eaten since the night before, and he is starting to feel hungry. He orders a full tourist breakfast: Radio Uno is paying, and he'll have no trouble expensing this one. A double espresso, orange juice (in a bottle: disgusting), croissants . . . for nearly eleven euros. A tourist price, too. It's almost time for his appointment. Once more, Diego checks the street number where he has to be in five minutes, and then starts down the stairs, feeling the adrenaline kick in. He doesn't know yet who he is going to meet or what the person will tell him, only that it will be critically important. Standing outside number 55 rue Lamarck is an old woman leaning on a cane. When Diego nears, she looks up at him, smiles, and speaks to him directly in Spanish.

"Diego Martin? Good morning, I am Emilia Ferrer, Isabel's grandmother."

He never saw that one coming. He guessed the lawyer had arranged for him to meet an older individual, someone who had lived under Franco, maybe someone who had been a victim of El Caudillo's police. But her own grandmother? He begins to understand Isabel Ferrer's involvement with the National Association of Stolen Babies. He is so surprised that he forgets to greet the woman, who is still planted firmly in front of him. She bursts into laughter.

"Well, don't just stand there like an idiot! I see my granddaughter didn't warn you. . . . I thought she should, but she persuaded me to let it be a surprise. Judging from the look on your face, it certainly was."

"Excuse me, yes, you're right, I . . . Let me just say, with my apologies, good morning, ma'am, and thank you."

"Knock it off with your 'ma'am's;' none of that between us! Call me Emilia," says the old woman with a wink. "Now, let's go up to the apartment. I'll make you a coffee, and we'll have a talk. I'm guessing you have some questions. And I have some answers, but above all, I have quite a story to tell you."

An old-fashioned elevator with heavy black steel doors carries them slowly to the fifth floor. Emilia doesn't say another word the whole way up, but she never takes her eyes off the journalist. Only a smile that breaks over her face as he gropes nervously in his bag for his Nagra and headphones and presses the record button after she signals to him with a quick movement of her hand and a nod to start. Once inside her tidy two-bedroom apartment, Diego can't resist the temptation to take a good look around. The apartment is bright and furnished in a tastefully contemporary style, something else he didn't expect. No heavy wood sideboards or antique dressers here. No; the beige and white minimalist interior might have been lifted right from a furniture showroom. Anticipating his question, she explains that her granddaughter redecorated the apartment for her a few months ago after Emilia's husband passed away.

Seated now in the living room, with a pitcher of water, two glasses, an Italian espresso pot, and two steaming cups before them on the stylish glass coffee table, the journalist and the grandmother have not yet begun their interview. Diego likes to take his time, soak up the atmosphere, and wait to have the undivided attention of his subject before launching into his first question. Next to the flat-screen TV that faces the white leather couch where they are sitting, a writing table holds a black-and-white photo of a youngish-looking man in a suit and a Panama hat, his head thrown back in laughter. He is standing in a wide, public square surrounded by pigeons that look to be pestering him.

"Is that your husband?" Diego asks, indicating the picture.

"Yes, that is my Vicente. I love that photo. It was so long ago, just after our wedding; we went to Valencia for our honeymoon. A different time. He died about a year ago; his cancer had spread. But he's always with me. I visit him once a week. He's nearby, at the Montmartre cemetery."

"He didn't want to be buried in Spain?"

"Absolutely not! We never went back after we left. That was in 1946. Let's get started, shall we? Ask me your first question; I'll do my best to help you understand what happened to us and why we fled our country."

Two hours of questions and answers. Diego is exhausted, and he can tell that Emilia is too. She spoke for most of that time. She told her story, simply, directly, and emotionally, and she never let up. She has great resolve, but at eighty-nine and in fragile health, this trip back in time has taken a toll on her. She asks Diego to pass her a pill box and serves herself from it with a large glass of water. Her breathing is labored, which worries the journalist. He doesn't want to leave her like this.

"Are you sure you don't want to call your doctor? I'll stay with you until he arrives."

"No, no, I'm fine. It's just that it's the first time I ever told any-one all of that at once. I didn't think it would affect me so much. I'm going to lie down for a moment. I'm sure I'll feel better then. Don't worry," Emilia says, seeing Diego's concern. "I just have one thing to ask you."

"Of course. What is it?"

"Make good use of my story: broadcast it, and talk about it. I can assure you that I am convinced that I am not the only woman this happened to. That's why my granddaughter took up the cause of the NASB. The public has to know about this scandal. And whoever did this is going to have to pay."

"I'll do my best." Diego hesitates. "You're aware, however, that before I do, I'm going to have to verify quite a lot of this. You are making some serious allegations. I have to look into them more closely. But rest assured I will help you. Our interview will air on my next show, and it's going to drop like a bomb."

"So much the better!"

"Which makes me wonder . . . Are you sure you want to go through with this? There might be some unwelcome repercus-sions. I won't name you on my show, but my colleagues might come looking for you. Other journalists are going to want to meet you, and it won't be hard to find you."

"I'm not worried!" Emilia reassures the journalist. "Anyways, this is the only interview I'm giving. I've done my part. Now it's up to you and Isabel to do yours."

Her last comment strikes Diego as odd, and it sticks with him as he boards the train back to the airport. Before that, though, he took a detour to the cemetery to find the final resting place of Vicente Ferrer, Emilia's husband. Not far from the grave of the singer Dalida, he located Vincente's sober tombstone, decorated only by a bouquet of flowers. On it were inscribed his name, birth date, date of death, and a sentence that has the ring of a rallying cry: *"¡No pasarán!"* Clearly a staunch supporter of the left and an early anti-Francoist.

Diego has four hours until his flight, but he wants to sit down in one of the airport bars to gather his thoughts, take some notes in his Moleskine, and listen to the tape recording. He gets up incessantly to smoke cigarette after cigarette near the taxi stand outside. No one seeing him pacing back and forth with his headphones on would guess he was listening to anything other than music. In reality, he is making himself travel back through the years with Emilia a second time, to suffer again through her heartbreaking story. The story of a young wife, twenty-one years old, who was excitedly expecting a child. The baby would be born in a country that a brutal dictator kept subjugated under his iron fist, but he would be welcomed by loving parents. They were active members of the Communist Party and fervent opponents of the regime. They had considered very seriously before making the decision to start a family. They had been baited, arrested, and even tortured by Franco's men. But they remained hopeful that Franco would be overthrown one day. When Emilia's water broke, she was alone. Her husband was at a secret meeting to plan strategic attacks on several government buildings. A friend took her to the maternity ward, in a hospital operated by the Catholic

Church, as so many hospitals were at the time. But there, everything that could go wrong did. When the nuns and the midwives explained to her that her baby boy died during delivery, her life changed forever.

The utmost discretion was required for this meeting, so David Ponce asked Isabel to meet him at Casa Pepe, his and Diego's preferred lunch spot. The owner, a friend, agreed to close up earlier than usual, no questions asked. At nine o'clock, he simply pulled the roll-down gate over the entrance and left the keys with the judge, along with a few plates of tapas. Now David and Isabel are the only ones in the restaurant. Before getting started, Isabel informs him that she put Diego in touch with her grandmother and tells David her story in a few sentences. He is surprised but doesn't let it show, nor does he give a hint of the effect the young woman's beauty and intensity are having on him. She seems to be motivated by both an iron will and an unquenchable desire for justice. Does her sense of indignation stem from the wrong done to her family? That attitude could prove dangerous: there's a fine line between justice and revenge, David thinks. His fears are swept aside, however, when she produces a pile of documents, mostly originals, some very old, some more recent, as well as transcriptions of statements by mothers whose children were forcibly taken from them.

The judge reads in silence. Isabel is prepared to give him all the time he needs. She doesn't want to sway him in any way. She nibbles at the tapas, pours herself a glass of wine, then another, and smokes one cigarette after the other. His attention absorbed entirely by the file, David doesn't eat anything or even taste his beer. From time to time, he writes something down in a little notebook. After an hour like this—an eternity for the lawyer— he raises his gaze at last and looks Isabel straight in the eyes. He takes a deep gulp of his beer, picks up his pack of Peter Stuyvesants (the last person in Madrid to still smoke them), and finally addresses her in a tone of voice that he hopes sounds casual but that belies his excitement.

"Why me?"

She was expecting this question and has her response ready.

"Because you have the experience and you are highly respected, and because you have already investigated some very complicated political cases, because—"

"I'll repeat the question: Why did you choose me? And don't give me your prepared speech; I want the truth."

"OK, OK . . . You're right. I'll give you the short, simple answer. Why you? Because, as far as I can tell, you are the only judge with the cojones to open an investigation, you don't give a damn about the fallout, and, if what they say about you at the courthouse is true, you're a first-class pain in the ass."

"See? That wasn't so hard," replies David. "Well, thanks, first of all. I'll take that as a compliment. Second, it's clear from what you've just shown me that I could start a preliminary investigation. However, my superiors in the department will block me at every step. The families are going to have to press charges, but will they? And if they do, do they understand what that could mean? For both them and for the country? If all of this is true, this is not simply a case of human trafficking but of an entire system put in place to kidnap children, and one that functioned for years and years. I'm not even talking about the underlying ideology here. As for you, no one who takes aim at the halls of power gets away unscathed."

"They're ready, they understand the risks; I've been through it all with them. And don't worry about me. I know what I'm doing and whose toes I'm stepping on."

"Fine. I'll call you in twenty-four hours with my decision."

"No, I'll call you. I hope you'll make the right choice. In the meantime, if you don't mind, these documents are going to stay with me. If you need them, you know where to find them. And if you decide to help us, I think I can find you more like them, too."

Isabel gets up from the table, slowly gathers her things, and stops for a moment in front of David. After a minute during which she sizes him up intently with her dark eyes, she extends her hand to him, then walks out without a word of goodbye. He leans back on the banquette for a long moment. Eventually, he decides to clear the table and moves behind the bar to make himself a coffee. He spies a bottle of Cognac above the espresso machine, grabs it, and pours a generous shot into his coffee cup. He sits back down at the table, opens his notebook, and rereads what he wrote down earlier. His mind is made up already. The answer is yes, and David is even going to offer to file the first complaints himself. Hard to know what will happen next. His career will undoubtedly take a detour, but he can handle it. On the other hand, the scandal that is brewing is going to be nothing short of explosive. The consequences of an affair this big are unpredictable, especially when the highest-ranking positions in government are filled by people whose own families orchestrated the kidnappings. There are no guarantees of winning this one.

Isabel strides quickly through Malasaña's bustling streets. People are everywhere. Young and old, all with glasses in hand. An indescribable din fills the air of Madrid's trendiest neighborhood. Nightclubs with their doors wide open are pumping a mix of musical styles (electro, rumba, disco) onto the sidewalks, which may as well be a giant disco. She parked her car nearby. Lost in thought—she is disappointed that the judge didn't say yes immediately, but she is holding out hope that he will—she does not notice that a man is following her from a distance of about fifty feet. He waited for her in a car parked outside Casa Pepe and started tailing her when she left. Dressed in black pants and a black jacket, he walks silently with his hands in his pockets as he gets closer. When she opens her car door, he is right next to her, with a ski mask over his face. He grabs her violently, throws her face-first against the hood of the car, and keeps her in that position so she can't see him. With one hand, he takes a fistful of her hair and with the other covers her mouth to prevent her from calling for help. Frozen with fear, Isabel doesn't dare move. She thinks her attacker is going to rape her, but when he brings his mouth close to her ear, she understands what's happening.

"This is your first warning," he tells her in a cold, hard whisper. "You can see for yourself: we're following you, we know who you are, and we know what you do. If you want to stay alive, this is where you turn back. Put an end to this association and its lies about stolen babies. If not . . ."

He gives Isabel a violent blow to the head such that she almost loses consciousness, then he runs off, disappearing into one of the crowded pedestrian streets.

At the same time, two men in a delivery van parked directly behind Isabel's car have watched the whole incident play out. They even filmed it and took pictures. One of them wanted to jump in at first, but his partner stopped him.

"No! That's not what we're here for! Our job is only to keep an eye on her, take pictures, write a report, and see what the chief says. But Jesus! Who is that bastard? He didn't steal anything. It's got to have something to do with the NASB. We're going to have to let HQ know right away. We're not the only ones in this business, apparently."

Isabel is still paralyzed with shock. She remains slumped over the hood for a long time before she is sure she can turn herself over. Her head is killing her. When the fear finally drains from her, she tells herself as she gets behind the wheel of her car that this was only child's play. The worst is yet to come. But it is going to take more than that to frighten her. She hasn't yet finished what she started. And she plans to see this to the end.

9

IT'S ALMOST TIME for *Radio Confidential* to start. Diego locks his office, checks that he has all the documents he'll need while he's on the air, and takes the elevator to the basement, earlier than usual. He doesn't meet anyone on the way. It's as if the entire station was on standby. It's Friday night, so most of Radio Uno's employees have left for the weekend. *Radio Confidential*'s producer is already in the control room of Studio 4, his attention moving from the soundboard to a computer screen to the potentiometers to the cue sheet, preparing all of the sound cues he'll use during the show.

"¡*Hola!*" Diego shouts out as he bursts into the studio.

"Christ! You scared the shit out of me! What, you're here already? What gives? Are you sick or something?"

"Nope. I just thought that, for once, I'd get here early. Also, I have to talk to you—there have been some changes. You can throw out the running order sheet I gave you before. I made a new one."

"Oh, shit! And you're only telling me now? You're a real jackass, you know that?"

"Now, just take a look," Diego says. "We're going to start with this, and then, after Prosecutor X, we're going to go right into this interview."

Diego hands a flash drive and the new running order sheet to his producer, who starts to read it. He sighs deeply.

"Umm, my friend . . . Are you sure this is what you want to do? Do the studio execs know?"

"One hundred percent sure. And no, I didn't tell anyone. In any case, there's no one here now; who could I tell on a Friday at eleven thirty at night? Don't worry! Look, I'll take the blame for everything, like always. But they'll only make a big deal out of it to look tough, given the audiences we're going to have."

"It's your call," says his producer incredulously. "What the hell do I care? They can't fire me; I'm a union rep. But you, you're playing with fire here."

"Yeah, yeah. We'll just see. Let's go now: get this interview into your machine there. You ain't seen nothin' yet. I'm going to get set up in the studio. And I'm counting on you not to make any calls before the show starts. They've got quite a surprise in store for them."

Before taking his seat at the microphone and getting his headphones on, Diego makes a quick stop at the coffee machine. He doesn't really need the caffeine, but he could use an ashtray. He presses the button for hot water and carries the steaming plastic cup into the studio. As soon as the heavy door swings shut, he lights a cigarette. From the other side of the window, the producer shoots him a nasty look and, to express the extent of his disapproval, gives Diego the finger too, but it only provokes a burst of laughter from the journalist.

Diego picks up his notes and reads through his script one last time. He can feel his excitement building as the hour approaches for launching the show, which is now less than ten minutes away. All that's left to do is post a summary of the upcoming show to social media. Twitter and Facebook will spread the information in a matter of seconds, and Diego's followers will share it and tune into Radio Uno. He prepared a tweet and a text for Facebook before coming into the studio. It just takes a click to send them out. Finally, he texts his live guest. This is a little surprise he kept from his producer: "Phone call to" is all that he wrote on the new running order sheet. His guest's number is saved onto Diego's phone. "I'll call you in the final ten minutes of the show, so be ready." It will be late by that time, but this story will be on everyone's lips tomorrow.

The show begins. Opening music. Lead-in. Announcement: a special edition on the stolen babies scandal, with an exclusive interview. Followed by Prosecutor X's segment, and its usual shockwaves. After that and the musical break ("Chinga Tu Madre" [Screw Your Mother] by the Mexican group Molotov— Diego has a flair for irony), he gets into the evening's topic. He gives a quick summary of the affair to date and a reminder of the NASB's activities and then breaks the suspense by signaling to his producer to launch his interview with Emilia Ferrer. Just as Diego promised her, he never uses her last name or mentions her location, revealing only that they met "somewhere in France."

For twenty minutes, the elderly woman's voice is the only sound there is in the studio. The emotion is palpable. Even the producer wipes tears from his eyes as he hangs on her every word.

"I was exhausted. My water had broken twelve hours earlier, and the baby still hadn't come. My husband either. He had left the day before for work, and he didn't even know I was at the maternity ward. This was in 1946. Communication wasn't as easy as it is now. I was lying there alone in the delivery room. I was in pain. I was crying. Every once in a while, a nun came by to see how I was doing. She never told me her name. I do remember, though, that she was very young. In fact, she only worried me more, telling me that the labor had been very long and that the baby could be harmed if it continued. I was in a panic. Finally, I delivered, in great pain. I heard my baby cry. He was alive when he was born and in perfect health, I know that. A mother knows those things. I know it, that's all I can say. The nun took him as soon as the doctor cut the umbilical cord. She never even let me hold him; I only had a glimpse of his little face. She left the room, and I never saw my son again. After what seemed like an eternity, the young nun returned, alone. She took my hand and explained to me that my baby wasn't doing well when he finally arrived and that was the reason that she

took him out so quickly, to try to save him. And that they tried everything, but he died, unfortunately. That I would have to be very brave. That she was there for me. That it was a hardship. That I would get over it. That I would have other children. I screamed. I beat the table with my arms. I tried to get up. They wouldn't let me. They even tied me down. There were a few of them: the nun, a doctor, and some nurses. I cried and cried and cried for hours. I yelled at them to give me my baby back. That they were lying, that he was alive, that I had to see him. The nun told me that was impossible. That it was better not to. That I needed to rest. A doctor came in and gave me a shot of something. I fell asleep. When I woke up, my husband was there, red-eyed, holding my hand. I yelled again that they had stolen my baby. My husband didn't know what to do, he didn't understand. Of course, when he got to the hospital, they told him the baby had died. They gave me another sedative, a powerful one. It went on like that for several days, until I was well enough to go home and they could get rid of me. I told my husband everything that happened. He didn't want to believe me at first, but then he started to listen more carefully to what I was saying. But it was too late. There was nothing we could do. He went back to the maternity ward several times to try to get to the bottom of it. Nothing. They just told him the same thing. When I was discharged, they gave me an official document, a death certificate, and a certificate of burial. They pointed us to a grave in the cemetery near the hospital, where they said my son was buried. I'm sure it's empty. My son cannot be there for the simple reason that he didn't die. I don't know what they did with him, but I know he is alive and that he was perfectly healthy when he came into the world. They stole my baby. And today, I think to myself that I'm not the only one this happened to. When I heard about the NASB, it was like a light bulb went on. Everything came back to the surface. I am convinced that other mothers have suffered the same ordeal. Whoever did this must be punished."

While the interview aired, the switchboard at Radio Uno lit up. The phone lines jammed, and messages from listeners poured onto the show's Facebook page and Twitter feed. In the studio, Diego was eating it up: bull's-eye! The two young interns whose job it is to screen callers didn't know where to start. They tried their best to verify the identities of the callers before dashing off a line on each for the journalist. During the call-in hour that followed, the reactions were endless. They came mostly from women who wanted to thank Emilia for her courageous testimony, or who said they lived through the same horror, convinced like Emilia that their babies were alive and that they had been kidnapped. Other callers had stories about strange things that happened on the maternity ward where Emilia gave birth. Men called in, too, younger men, to share on the air their suspicions about their parents: "What if I'm one of the stolen babies?" they wondered aloud.

Diego had never imagined so many calls would come in with stories similar to Emilia's, which confirmed what he'd read in the documents Isabel Ferrer had given him. However, he's still missing an essential piece of the puzzle: the motivation. Why kidnap children? For whom? To do what? Diego won't let himself believe it was just for the money. But then, why not? Nothing that happens in this country can surprise him anymore.

"Thanks to everyone who called in," he says into the microphone. "We're almost out of time. But before we wrap up this special edition—which is only the first of many, I assure you—I'd like to open our lines to one final caller, who has an announcement to make. Judge David Ponce, good evening. I'm guessing that what you heard tonight only corroborates your decision?"

"Good evening, and thank you for the opportunity to speak tonight. Of course, like everyone else listening this evening, I'm shaken, devastated even. But putting my feelings aside, in the wake of the launch of the NASB and having seen a certain number of documents that the association's lawyer made available to me—I won't call them proof yet—I have decided to open a special investigation into the abduction, illegal confinement, and trafficking of minors. I can't tell you yet where this investigation will lead, but our justice system owes answers to these families."

Kaboom. The second bomb of the night, which had been kept under wraps right up until it detonated. He had seen David Ponce's message when he got back from Paris, describing his meeting with

Isabel Ferrer. "We have to talk," the text said. And that's how Diego became the first person to learn of the judge's decision.

"I'm going to make a motion to open a preliminary inquiry: there's too much in what she showed me. It's insane. She told me she had plenty more evidence and other people who wanted to come forward. We're talking about an entire system put into place by Franco's regime. Can you believe it? They were abducting kids and selling them!"

"You know you're taking a huge risk, don't you? Remember what you went through with the Castro case? That's going to be nothing compared to this, if you want my opinion."

"I know, I know. But Isabel Ferrer came to me with this: she came to me. If I don't do this, I'll never forgive myself. Sure, it's going to be tough. And with their damned amnesty, I don't have much recourse, but we'll try to get them for crimes against humanity if nothing else. It's a fail-safe and will get me around the law. At least, I hope so."

Announcing his decision on a Friday night was supposed to buy the judge some time before all hell broke loose. However, in a scandal of such proportions, the reactions are similarly excessive. David is still on the air when he receives a message from the Ministry of Justice. A summons to appear first thing the next morning. An independent judiciary? He's almost tempted to put the question to Diego's audience, while he still has the microphone, but decides against it.

Diego is dripping with sweat as he closes the show. Rarely has an episode of *Radio Confidential* been so intense. With the nighttime program launched, he stays in the studio for a few minutes by himself. The producer was so shocked by what he heard that he ran out as soon as he was finished. Diego needs a moment of quiet. It doesn't last long. His telephone won't stop ringing: Ana, the station's directors, Ponce, and some unknown numbers. Until he has caught his breath, he prefers not to answer. Two messages arrive simultaneously, each a single word: "Thanks." One is from Emilia, and the other is from Isabel. Mission accomplished. For tonight, at least.

He has really done it this time. Diego has to admit he's rather pleased with himself. What will happen next is anyone's guess, but one thing is for sure: it's only the beginning. In a country where unemployment is rising, factories are shutting, and businesses are going bankrupt, where no one trusts the political class and the years of dictatorship have left gaping wounds, the ruling party runs enormous risks, and even more so in this time of polarizing tensions. But they are going to do whatever it takes to maintain the status quo, to prevent any information from surfacing that could threaten this fragile democracy, this constitutional monarchy established by an aging tyrant and approved by the people because they were backed into a corner and had no other choice, less than forty years ago. In a country that idealizes children, kidnapping babies is a capital offense. If the king's subjects finally woke up, they could do some damage. Some serious damage.

Isabel is still in a state of shock from the attack. Her first reflex when she got home was to lock the door behind her and check the apartment for any signs of burglary or tampering; she looked for microphones too. After pouring herself a generous glass of red wine, she considered calling her grandmother but told herself it was better not to worry her. She decides to call Ana Durán. Isabel doesn't know why, but she feels she can trust Ana. The private detective reassures Isabel as best she can and offers to find her a bodyguard, but Isabel refuses.

"No, I'm not afraid of them. I'm just a bit shaken up; I wasn't expecting that already. I knew I might run into that kind of trouble, but it's something else entirely when it happens to you."

"If that's what you want, but be careful. Look behind you and keep an eye on who is around you in the street and the cars following you. In other words, be a bit more paranoid than usual. I'm not at all surprised that someone has you under surveillance. You know the government has unlimited means, and it won't hesitate to use them. We've already seen it in different circumstances."

"I'm going to take a break for a few days. Get out of Madrid. Turn off my phone and catch my breath on the coast."

"I don't know if it's such a good idea for you to disappear like that again. Don't stay away for too long. People will start asking questions. Anyways, we need you here."

"I'll be back in two days. I'll call you when I'm on my way."

Next stop: Valencia. It's March, so the third largest city in the country is currently buzzing, celebrating the arrival of spring with its annual Falles celebration. This local tradition dating back to the Middle Ages attracts millions of people. Huge papier-mâché tableaux lampooning events and personalities from the previous year will be burned in a giant pyrotechnic celebration amidst firecrackers and fireworks. This ephemeral outdoor art display goes up in flames with a terrifying din. It's not the ideal place to get some rest, but if your purpose is to go unnoticed, it's perfect. Isabel knows this only too well.

It's not a coincidence, either, that her travel plans coincide exactly with the one year anniversary of both the elections that brought the APM to power and her assassination of Paco Gómez. She has an appointment with an elderly woman who chose to retire in this Mediterranean city. The woman will die here, too, earlier than she planned, probably. When she does, Isabel will have terminated her mission.

Target number five is a woman. Isabel wonders if that might make this one any different, but she doesn't have the time to overthink it. She is going to have to act fast and in public. She followed some of Ana's advice and took precautions before coming to Valencia. In an attempt to throw off anyone who might be tempted to tail her, Isabel made several train reservations for various cities on different days and at different times. Then she rented a car to drive to Valencia. Her plan worked. The two men in the delivery van parked outside her apartment got word that she had made several train reservations. All they had to do was watch for her to leave to know which train she would be taking. When, to their surprise, they saw her leave by car for the station, they decided not to take any unnecessary risks by following her. Instead, they drove straight to the station to catch up with her there. Except she never showed up.

"Shit! She got us!" was all one of the agents could say.

Before he could reply, his colleague had to answer the phone. The director of the intelligence agency was on the line in person and expecting news. When he learned they had lost her, he was more than a little disappointed.

"Figure this out however you want, but find her, goddammit! You're useless! Unbelievable! I don't want to know your plan, just get her back in your sights!"

"Yes, sir. Thank you, sir. We'll be in touch."

Their job just got a lot more complicated. Where to begin? A regular needle in a haystack, this one. After checking her recent online purchases, they decide to split up: one leaves for Barcelona, the other for Valencia.

Valencia, Spain's orange capital, is only four hours by car from Madrid. Isabel is walking with the crowds that have taken over the central square in front of City Hall. This is the main stage of the festivities and the place to come to witness any of the Falles processions. Every afternoon at two o'clock, a match is put to a highly sophisticated pyrotechnic installation, launching a concert of fireworks across the city that would drown out a hundred Airbus jets taking off. That's the Mascletà. And it's completely insane. The noise is so loud that anyone watching has to stand with their mouths open to keep their eardrums from exploding. Hundreds of decibels make the earth shake for four minutes. The perfect cover for shooting someone. Isabel is convinced no one could possibly hear a gunshot in all the noise, which is why she decided to come here despite the risks.

While she waits to put the final step of her plan into action, she checks out the location, her camera in hand like every other tourist. She walks the perimeter of the square and then wanders into the maze of tiny pedestrian streets that lend the city its old-world charm. Across from the imposing Art Deco facade of City Hall stands another towering building from the same period, which houses the central post office. Next to that is a stone chapel with a wooden door. Pedestrians walk past without ever suspecting what's inside. Only the locals know that an enormous cloister lies just behind its walls, home to a Carmelite convent established here over a century ago.

Isabel pushes the door open and enters. She isn't here to pray but to scout out the location, although she considers whether lighting a candle would bring her luck. She read on the Internet and in several books that a back entrance exists that leads out onto a street on the other side of the post office. That is going to be her exit, and she wants to make sure it is open and will be tomorrow as well. She won't have long to get out, and she can't leave anything to chance. Her last hit is the hardest to set up, and there is no margin for error.

The night was short, and sleep was elusive. Revelers in the street below her window kept her up until early morning. Isabel dawdles in the neighborhood until one o'clock in the afternoon, when she takes up position in the chapel. She finds a seat in the back where she can observe the movements of the nuns and the chapel's few visitors. If they were to notice her, they would presume she was deep in prayer. She is looking for her target. Not so easy when the sisters wear identical habits. Several times she thinks she has spotted the one she is looking for before realizing her mistake. She starts to lose patience. Her frustration mounts as the hour of the Mascletà draws near.

Suddenly, a small group of nuns leaves the sacristy and makes their way to the back of the chapel where Isabel is seated. She doesn't move a muscle. Her eyes are riveted on the smallest one in the group, who is also the oldest. It's her. Sister Marie-Carmen. She walks with a sprightly gait for someone in her eighties. Isabel hears the nuns laughing as they walk past, moving toward the garden. Then the group splits up. Some return to their rooms, others stay in the chapel, near the stairs at the entrance. Sister Marie-Carmen sits on the low stone wall that borders the garden. Her feet barely touch the ground. She reaches into a pocket for her rosary and leans against a pillar. Isabel watches her every movement as the entire scene unfolds. In five minutes, the first fireworks will go off. She approaches slowly. For the time being, the nun is alone, which is a stroke of luck. But it may not last. Silently, Isabel inches closer. She is hidden now behind another pillar, only a dozen feet from her target, who has noticed nothing. The first burst of firecrackers outside makes Sister Marie-Carmen start. She smiles and returns to her rosary. *Now.* The noise from outside is deafening. Isabel looks left and right: no one. She steps out from behind the pillar and walks quickly toward the nun.

The sister raises her head just as Isabel points the gun at her. Before she can react, the noise of the gunshot dissolves into the detonations of the Mascletà. The lawyer catches Sister Marie-Carmen as she falls forward, then leans her body against the pillar, as if she were praying still. Her head rests on her chest, and a thin line of blood has stained her white-and-blue tunic. Less than thirty seconds later, Isabel walks out the back door and pushes her way through the crowd, the gun now stored neatly in her handbag. The Mascletà finishes with a closing salvo loud enough to rival a nuclear explosion and the public cries out and claps in approval.

Long after the crowds have dispersed, one of the two intelligence agents sent to keep an eye on Isabel is walking in the central square across from City Hall. He has been searching the streets of the historic city center since yesterday but with no luck. He knows she tricked him. It's a sign that Isabel suspects something is up. For now, he doesn't know what to do with himself. If he returns to Madrid without a single clue, his director is going to give him a royal dressing down. His colleagues' mockery will be even worse. He and his partner are going to be teased about this for weeks. When he finally gives up and heads back to Madrid, Isabel has already been home for hours.

10

IT'S A TSUNAMI. A media storm the likes of which the country has not experienced in years. In reality, it has never experienced anything like it. Or almost never. The only time Spain has been shaken like this was on February 23, 1981, the day of the attempted coup d'état, which was subdued less than twenty-fours after it began. Diego can still remember it. He was nine years old at the time. It was the first time he stayed up all night. He and his parents were glued to their transistor radio listening to live reports. That was probably when he decided he wanted to become a journalist. Today, Diego is the one in the eye of the hurricane. And he isn't the only one. Everyone is talking about his friend, David Ponce. The judge is in the hot seat. Rumors are flying, saying he's going to be fired. A first for the Ministry of Justice since the dictatorship. Other rumors say he might be charged with abuse of power and wrongdoing. In the gilded chambers where the government and the monarchy sit, David's show of support for the NASB could not have been greeted with any less enthusiasm. The minister of justice and the executive council of the Order of

Magistrates (which has never worn its name so well as it does now—clearly taking orders from the government) are invoking the Amnesty Law. No one in this country wants to even try to understand the actions of the past: they would rather close their eyes. No looking back, ever. The leaders of the regime—if they're still alive—and their descendants can rest easy. No one will trouble them or look into their affairs.

After Emilia's story aired on his show, Diego met up with Ana at her apartment. He didn't want to be alone. A drink would do him some good, preferably with someone he trusts. To talk about the scandal or to just get the scuttlebutt. Ever since Ana got involved with the NASB, they haven't seen each other much. But he knows she still has her ear to the ground for him. Tonight would be a good occasion for each of them to update the other on their separate investigations and to get the other's opinion. Ana always has good advice. Above all, her instincts are rarely wrong. Surprise: David Ponce was already there. He, too, needed someone to talk to tonight. So they share what they know, and what they're thinking: hypotheses, leads, stories, and so on. The judge gives them a detailed account of his meeting with Isabel. The journalist recounts his trip to Paris, and the private investigator enumerates everything she has seen and heard at the NASB's headquarters, including the news of Isabel's attack. They make a wily trio, and they enjoy each other's company—and many drinks—until the early hours of the morning.

Diego walks home. With his mind addled by fatigue and liquor, he is slow to react when someone dressed in black with a hoodie pulled down over his face accosts him a few feet from his building, blocking him from going any farther. The man doesn't say much, but he still is able to hurt Diego.

"Diego Martin?"

"Yes, what's this—?"

"Stop butting your nose in where it doesn't belong, you fucking muckraker!"

That's all the man says before doubling Diego over with a violent punch to the stomach. By the time Diego catches his breath and recovers his wits, his aggressor has vanished. Diego noticed something, however: the man was wearing a necklace with a pendant that resembled the Maltese cross. Diego was also struck by his voice, which was strangely gentle but firm at the same time and never rose into a yell.

As soon as Diego gets into his apartment, he calls Ana and David to warn them.

"Well, it's getting so we're going to have to watch our backs. Be careful, both of you, will you? That was just a friendly warning. Let's not let them make it worse."

"Don't worry," Ana reassures him. "We'll be ready for them."

Threats like these are common in their line of work. They have seen plenty of others. These attacks tell them one thing, though: they are making some people uncomfortable. Who? People in power, most likely, and they are starting to come out from the shadows. It's normal that the government would feel threatened by the accusations of the NASB, but who could be behind these threats? These aren't the preferred methods of the government's thugs, who usually apply pressure in much more subtle ways. They're going to have to widen their search.

Three days after the last explosive episode of *Radio Confidential*, the media is still covering the story 24/7, and the government is struggling to contain the fallout. The country has split in two. After the demonstrations set off by the economic crisis—to protest imposed austerity measures and draconian budget cuts to health care, in particular—even bigger and noisier ones are being announced in major cities. History's scars, so hastily bandaged, are opening into a gaping wound again.

Radio Uno, under fire from the Ministry of Communications, is also struggling to get a handle on the situation. Caught between a rock and a hard place, the station directors called Diego in to announce they are pulling him off the air for a week, a punishment that not only gives the station a black eye but will affect their ratings, as they well know. Pulling the show that just scored record audiences is hardly a smart business move. The numbers don't lie: over three million people tuned in during Emilia Ferrer's interview. And that's not even counting the hundreds of thousands more who downloaded the podcast. All told, over five million people listened to the show.

The Ministry of Justice is equally divided over the case of Judge David Ponce. The union that he presides over is reluctantly offering its support. In the corridors of the Audiencia Nacional, his colleagues are avoiding him. Better not to be seen with him, for now at least. The general consensus is that he is persona non grata. His meeting with the minister, which is said to have gone down violently, certainly didn't help his case. According to some sources who were present and who quickly leaked the information to the press, the two men nearly exchanged blows. Shouts and insults. Doors slamming. Neither one would listen to the other. The judge is expected to be dismissed, not in a few days but in a matter of hours. It will be a dramatic move, and it will only set people more on edge. The ship of state is sailing for rough seas. Mayday!

Making matters worse, David has been receiving death threats since he appeared on Diego's show. The old-fashioned way: a tiny wooden casket in his home mailbox. Another left at his office in the courthouse. Some more modern ones too. Dozens of emails. Offensive texts. "We're going to kill you!" "Next stop: the cemetery!" "Death to the traitor!" "You'll burn in Hell!" Some of them were sent by a fringe group going by the name of Francoists United. Others came from groups linked to Catholic extremists and people who were just nostalgic for the dictatorship. He filed complaints as a matter of principle, knowing nothing would come of it. He knows he doesn't have much time left before they show him the door, maybe only a matter of hours. To stay a step ahead of his superiors, he has already prepared and signed the paperwork to open an investigation for crimes against humanity, kidnapping, and child trafficking. No matter his fate, it will take several weeks for his request to be examined in full, which should give Isabel Ferrer enough time to gather more proof. His likely replacement will do what he's told until the Constitutional Court rules on the question. The judiciary apparatus has been officially set in motion. All he can do now is wait and pay the consequences—dearly, no doubt.

Too many people. Not enough room. A peculiar atmosphere has taken hold of the headquarters of the NASB. The offices are packed. People are standing and sitting anywhere they can. Both euphoria and anxiety hang in the air. The cheers of victory that greeted David Ponce's announcement have given way to fear. The staff celebrated that first step in the direction of truth and justice. But today, they are afraid. Afraid that the judge will be removed. Afraid that the inquiry will be dismissed. And afraid, above all else, for themselves. Over the last few days, anonymous letters have been arriving. No one paid them much attention initially. The members of the executive committee were expecting the association to receive hate mail. However, this is something else: letters have started to arrive at the homes of everyone who ever had any contact at all with the association. The same letter for everyone. But personalized. *"Dear (first name)."* Followed by an incoherent message:

> *"You were a Red Commie, you are a Red Commie, and you will die a Red Commie.*
>
> *Communist scum do not deserve to live or procreate. God protects His own. If He decided your child should die, then that's the way it is. And if you think he is alive,*

*which remains to be seen, know that the family that
raised him gave him more than you ever could."*

An emergency meeting has been called. Isabel, who came home
from Valencia the day before, asked Ana to come. The executive
committee's ten members are all present. Isabel's face is drawn as
she reveals to them that she was the victim of an attack, which
isn't the reassuring news they were hoping for.

"I have asked Ana to help us with this," Isabel continues. "We
were talking before the meeting, and she thinks that either we are
still experiencing fallout from the computer hack or, and this
would be worse, that we have been infiltrated by someone passing
themselves off as a volunteer. In any case, we know that our members' contact information has been stolen and that someone is
using it with the intention of silencing us."

No one says a word or looks at each other. A few people sigh,
and others hold their heads in their hands. Ana jumps in; she'd
rather not let their despair sink in if that's still possible at this
point.

"I want to start by saying that for the moment, we don't know
anything for sure. These are just hypotheses. No one on the executive committee is under suspicion, of course. If there is a leak, it's
not coming from here. On the other hand, let's be clear: I'm not
judging you, but I think that you were overwhelmed by everything that was happening early on, and because of the urgency of
the situation, you let everyone in who wanted to help. Everyone
and anyone at all, I'd go so far as to say. I've asked Isabel for her

permission, and if you all also agree, I want to check the backgrounds of the principal volunteers, starting with the ones who joined after the press conference. I'll need their names and contact information, from the entry-level receptionist to the most experienced IT specialist. It will take me a couple of days, so I'm counting on your discretion in the meantime. Not a word of this meeting to anyone else. And keep your eyes open; you never know."

After an update on the legal situation and the growing pile of new cases that have arrived since Emilia's interview aired, Isabel and Ana decide to continue their conversation outside, where they can speak freely. Until they know more about the origin of the leak, they have to take every precaution. What the lawyer didn't tell the executive committee, so as not to frighten them even more, is that she has also received death threats at home. Exactly like the ones David Ponce received. The noose is tightening. She is going to have to move faster.

In the main room at headquarters, one of the computer programmers who offered his services the day of the hack and who stayed on to manage the tech operations hasn't missed a beat of what has been happening in the office. Although he doesn't know what was disclosed at the meeting, judging from the worried expressions on the faces of the committee members as they exited the room, he can guess that his plan is paying off. He turns his computer off and excuses himself to take a cigarette break. He tries to listen in on some of the conversations around him but decides it's safer not to; he doesn't want to attract any attention.

When he is out on the sidewalk, he switches the SIM card in his phone and dials a number that he knows by heart.

"Father?"

"Yes, my son, what is it?"

"They're panicking. The letters are getting to them. The lawyer isn't doing any better, judging from the look on her face. What should I do now?"

"Good, very good. Come for your instructions tonight; same time, same place as the other day. In the meantime, don't do anything except watch and listen."

"Yes, Father. See you tonight."

"May God bless you."

11

IN THE MIDST of all this chaos, news has arrived that is diverting attention from the stolen babies: a nun has been murdered in Valencia. Diego is on it, of course. To tell the truth, he has some time on his hands. Since he was pulled off the air, he hasn't left his apartment except for food, cigarettes, and coffee at Casa Pepe. He's making the best of the situation to get some rest and has declined all invitations from the press, particularly the television stations, who wanted him to come on to "debate" the topic of the stolen babies. With Ana's help, however, he has managed to get an appointment with Isabel Ferrer for the next day. Until then, he's taking it easy. Putting the case aside for a day or two, he'll be able to think more clearly when he comes back to it. He has also used the time to get caught up on his current obsession, *True Detective*. With everything happening lately, he has already missed half of the first season.

He has also allowed himself to surf the Internet for information on this latest murder. Browsing from site to site, Diego lost track of how he got to *Levante*, one of Valencia's two regional dailies. Maybe he was looking for a video of the Falles festival, which has just ended. His wife Carolina loved the Falles. They went many times, although he would drag his feet because he found the racket of the Mascletà to be intolerable. But he always gave in to her. And he had to admit, he liked the energy of this city that closed its streets to traffic and became an immense open-air bar. He was still playing the memories in his head as he stared at the headline on the paper's home page: "Who Gunned Down a Nun During the Falles? Our Exclusive Investigation." He starts clicking on all the articles he can find, including a long one on Sister Marie-Carmen's background. A Carmelite sister expertly assassinated during the Mascletà—there's a story there, for sure. And one that is sure to become a topic on his show very soon. An unusual murder and little to nothing known about it except that the old nun was discovered in the cloister, shot in the head. The presumed time of death, according to the coroner and the statements of the other sisters, coincides exactly with the Mascletà. As for a motive, the police have come up empty.

He calls Ana to talk about this latest murder and to ask her to see what she can find out. The detective currently has her hands full running background checks on the NASB's volunteers.

"Yes, I saw that. It'll make quite a story for you, now that you mention it. Hold on! What did you say the sister's name was?"

"Sister Marie-Carmen. Why?"

"I'm not sure, but the name sounds familiar. I feel like I've seen it somewhere. Give me some time to finish this job first, and then I'll get on it."

"OK, keep me posted. That would be bizarre, don't you think? It would make a great show, though," says Diego before switching gears. "What are you working on, something to do with the NASB?"

"Yep, I thought so. And, yeah, it's those anonymous letters. Do you remember, I mentioned them to you in passing? If you ask me, the NASB had all their information stolen when their site was hacked just after the press conference. These people are nice and hard-working, but when it comes to security, they're total amateurs. I just want to be sure they haven't been infiltrated by some nutcase fascist, or worse."

"Don't be too hard on them. The volunteers are doing their best. After everything they've been through, it's pretty brave of them to pick this fight. I mean, have you noticed the pandemonium they've created? At the same time, they're doing the right thing; they can't give up. You'll let me know if you find anything out?"

"Of course!" says Ana. "Listen, I'll see you tomorrow. I'm going to accompany Isabel to your meeting. I just want to be sure she gets there safe and sound."

"You think she could be the target of another attack?"

"She's been roughed up once already, and she's received death threats like David. And then, the other day when I was with her, I had the impression we were being followed. I didn't say anything so as not to frighten her, but tomorrow I want to make sure. If we can prevent the intelligence services or whoever this is from showing up at our favorite bar, that would be a good thing, don't you think?"

"Agreed. I'm going to see how David is doing. Oh, since you mention him, he's boiling mad and pretty sure he's going to be fired."

In his office at the courthouse, Judge Ponce is packing his belongings into boxes. A final decision has yet to be handed down, but he has been summoned to appear in two days before the governing board of magistrates. Undoubtedly, to receive his dismissal. His altercation with the minister of justice was the last straw. His immediate superior has already removed him from several cases, and the few journalists with whom he has developed a purely professional relationship—Diego is different—have heard rumors that he will indeed be removed from the bench. The question in David's mind is how this will happen exactly. Judges aren't just fired; there has to be a damn good reason. It wouldn't be impossible for them to try to stick him with something that would force him to quit. But he would never quit. Never. There aren't a lot of avenues for pressuring him either: he's single, has no wife or kids, and has no other family members except a brother he hasn't spoken to for years. Their only recourse, in his opinion, is a disciplinary hearing. After that, he can say adios to the Audiencia Nacional. So he has decided to await the final verdict patiently, even with a certain serenity. He already has a plan for what he'll do after they show him the door.

Ana has been reading so many names on so many different kinds of documents, she can hardly see straight anymore. But ever since

Diego mentioned the murdered nun, she can't stop thinking about it and has put aside the fastidious work of checking the NASB files to take a look through her own. She's been at it for an hour already, turning her office inside out, firing up her hard drive and going through every file related to any investigation she has ever done. Nothing. No Sister Marie-Carmen anywhere. Discouraged, she throws herself onto the dark brown leather recliner that sits like a throne in front of the window and looks one last time around the tiny room that serves as the headquarters of her detective agency, Ana & Associates. Still nothing. It's possible she was mistaken. She tells herself that her memory is starting to fail her, which won't be good for business.

She decides to take a walk to see her former colleagues still hustling on Rue del Pez and have a drink with them. It's seven o'clock, a little early in the evening, but not unreasonably so. In any case, she has a long night ahead of her if she's going to get through all of the NASB files. Two hours later, after a few beers and a round of tapas with the girls, she gets back to her office, turns on the lights, wakes up her computer, and sits in front of it. Ana is just about to pick up her work where she left off when she accidentally pushes a pile of investigation reports off the edge of her desk. She picks one up and pages through it excitedly and then gives an elated shout:

"Holy shit, here it is! I knew it!" Ana says out loud as if someone was in the office to share the news with.

She grabs her phone to tell Diego. She wasn't mistaken; she did come across the name of Sister Marie-Carmen somewhere, in a case from a few months ago. Over the course of her investigation, she found several official documents mentioning the nun.

The day of her meeting with Diego Martin is finally here. Isabel is more nervous than she imagined she would be. Since he was the journalist who announced the opening of an official investigation under pressure from the NASB, she has decided he also gets to be the one to interview her. Her only interview. Her one and only media appearance, and she hopes it will be her last. Of course, there will still be occasional press releases and press conferences—where Isabel won't take any questions, just as when the NASB launched. There will be others, too, timed to respond to the Ministry of Justice's decisions, but she will always conduct them the same way: after reading an official statement, she will say thank you and goodbye to the ladies and gentleman of the press. The threats haven't let up, and the lawyer is struggling to manage the stress of it all. Since her attack in the street, Isabel has been plagued by nightmares and is only sleeping in fits and starts.

She was relieved when Ana offered to come with her to the meeting. The idea of being out alone late at night in Malasaña again, the same neighborhood where Isabel was assaulted, wasn't at all appealing to her. The detective should be here any minute. The meeting is to take place in the same bar where Isabel met Judge Ponce, which surprises her, but Ana explained that the judge and the journalist have made it their unofficial second office.

Isabel is ready. She has waited a long time for this moment, which she knows will lay the foundations for what is to come. She practiced what she wants to say, the message she wants to send out. She scribbled some bits of phrases on scrap paper, but she threw them out. Isabel would prefer to just answer the journalist's questions. She thinks it will look better if she appears natural and doesn't read from any prepared statements. After all, she knows this inside and out. She just needs to give an impression of strength, as she used to do when making her closing arguments to a jury. Above all, Isabel has to keep her emotions out of it. Her mantra is: just the facts, nothing but the facts, and only the facts. Repeating that to herself, she gets her things together.

It will take two people to carry the huge bag of incriminating documents that she plans to give to Diego. The witnesses have kept coming forward ever since Daniel and Josefa, two of the founding members of the NASB and whose stories were the impetus for creating the association, contacted her. They told her about the deathbed confession by a father to his son revealing that the son had been adopted, or rather bought, at the time of his birth, and about a mother who, like Emilia, is convinced that her child was taken from her just after she delivered. At first, there were about thirty stories in all. Today, the association has gathered several hundred, and the numbers are growing by the day. It won't be long before they reach a thousand. Isabel won't be able to continue on her own; she'll need reinforcements, and she plans to use the interview to advertise for help. What she didn't let herself believe is proving true: the number of abductions is staggering, and they took place over a stupefyingly long period of time. Isabel is still shocked by the realization. But the evidence is there. There are official documents that should leave no doubt in anyone's mind. This country allowed a veritable mafia to buy and sell children to the tune of millions.

Ana rings the bell.

"Are you ready?" she asks after giving Isabel a hug, her very Latin way of saying hello.

"Yes. Listen, can you help me with this? It's heavy."

"What is all that? Are you moving?" Ana asks.

"I made copies of all of my files for Diego. He has to understand the amplitude of this system."

"You know, I think he doesn't doubt that."

"Really, I believe you, but I think that he needs to immerse himself in it. It went on for so long that sometimes I wonder if it isn't still happening today."

"Are you serious?"

"I wonder sometimes, that's all. I have one case, a well-documented one too, from 2005."

"Jesus! That's crazy! Well, come on, let's go. Señor Diego is going to get impatient if we don't get a move on."

The two women fill the trunk of Isabel's car with the big bag full of papers, photos, and press clippings, and then they get in. On their way out of the parking garage, Ana notices a gray delivery van parked nearby but says nothing. It starts up as they pass, then follows from a safe distance, the length of one or two cars. It's a tail. Just as she suspected. The lawyer is under surveillance. No doubt about that anymore. Ana is going to have to squeeze some contacts to tell her who is behind it.

The women spend ten minutes trying to find a parking spot before Isabel loses patience and decides to leave the car at a crosswalk. It's after ten o'clock; there's not much risk of getting towed at this hour. From the looks of the sidewalks, which are covered haphazardly with parked cars, no one else cares much about getting a ticket either. As soon as she turns off the engine, the van comes alongside, brakes just when it is even with them, then starts up again, turns right, then right again, and takes up a position about fifty feet behind them, parking in front of the entrance to a garage and turning off its lights. Isabel didn't notice anything, but Ana caught every detail. The van has a tinted windshield and a tinted rear window. It's a surveillance vehicle for sure, either the police or the intelligence services.

Luckily for the two women, given the weight of the bag, the bar is close by. Casa Pepe's roll-down gate is locked. Isabel knocks, and Diego opens up the gate. Lawyer and journalist, face-to-face for the first time: awkward. Neither moves nor knows how to greet the other. Ana puts them out of their misery with a comical grimace.

"Oh my god! Look at the two of you! A couple of teenagers! Now, come on, say hello. It won't hurt you."

Isabel and Diego laugh, still rather too uncomfortable, but finally exchange a kiss on the cheek in greeting. Diego is the first to speak.

"Well, I think we have plenty to talk about," is all he can manage. He can't stop looking at Isabel, with her deep, dark eyes, her delicate features, and her elegance.

David Ponce had warned him: "She is a beautiful woman. Not so tall, but she exudes a rare blend of sensuality and class. Be careful you don't fall for her!"

"Yes, I'm sure you're right. I brought some things that might interest you," she answers, indicating the bag of papers at her feet.

With the introductions out of the way and the meeting beginning, Ana decides to leave them alone.

"I'm going to take off. You don't need me here while you talk and record the interview. Isabel, if you want, call me when you're ready to leave, and I'll come back to get you. I'll be in the neighborhood. I have a couple of things to take care of."

As soon as the detective is outside, she makes some phone calls, then goes to wait in another one of Malasaña's bars, where she knows the owner as well. It takes only a few minutes for Ana's phone to ring. The conversation is brief. When she hangs up, she leaves the bar and walks calmly toward the gray delivery van.

12

DOZENS OF PAPERS are spread across the length of the bar. Two nearby tables are similarly encumbered. Diego and Isabel didn't notice the time pass. The sun is coming up, and Carlos, Casa Pepe's owner, will be in soon to open. They are going to have to pack up before he can raise the roll-down gate and welcome the first clients of the day, the early risers, the ones whose jobs start at the crack of dawn, and also the insomniacs, clubbers, and partiers who need a strong coffee and something in their stomachs before going home to sleep off the night.

The two spent the night reading and rereading all the documents, checking and comparing their relevant facts. They started, however, by recording Isabel's interview, during which the lawyer demonstrated flawless composure and conviction. A little over two hours of sound that the journalist is going to have to cut and edit for his show. He still doesn't know when he'll be able to go live with it. If all goes well, he should be back on the air in a few days. That is unless Radio Uno's directors decide they like being the government's lap dog. Still, it would be hard to keep him off the air for another week. That means Diego could run it as early as Friday, the next regularly scheduled *Radio Confidential*. That would leave him less than forty-eight hours to finish his edit. Barring something unexpected, he could have a new scoop for the station directors. This time, though, he'll give them a heads-up. With a story like this, they wouldn't dare stop him, no matter how much it could hurt the ruling party. Even public radio cares about ratings, and they would rather get hauled over the coals than pass this one up. Moreover, the station directors know that Diego won't hesitate to break his exclusivity clause to take his story to a competitor. Plus, Diego would relish the opportunity to accuse the station of disregarding his protections under labor law. For once, the only thing they can do is pretend to offer their support. In any case, they aren't fooling anyone.

What the NASB is about to go public with, according to its spokesperson, could have grave consequences for the government, the monarchy, and even democracy itself. People are fed up. The economic crisis has been fanning tensions, and several anti-government demonstrations have degenerated into riots. For the moment, the first public marches in support of the NASB have taken place peacefully, with only a few hundred people in attendance. However, if the size of the protests grows, which Isabel anticipates, given the number of cases arriving daily at the NASB, there could be clashes with the police. Already, the country's security forces are on edge. Moreover, some military generals are warning about the chaos reigning in the country, a chilling reminder of the 1981 coup d'état. Also, legislators have voted in a law authorizing police officers to fire on citizens "in case of imminent danger to order and security." Such a statement permits a wide margin for interpretation.

Isabel made her statement, too. While speaking at length. And eloquently, at that. Without ever raising her voice but leaving no doubt with her tone that she will pursue this to the end, Isabel demanded justice for these mothers, fathers, sisters, brothers, and entire families who are looking for answers, and who need to know the truth and want to see those who are responsible for their pain arrested and tried. Her argument is unequivocal and resonates without the slightest hesitation into Diego's headphones.

"When the NASB's two founders, Josefa and Daniel, came to me with their stories, I thought at first that they were fairly typical: a paternity suit and a kidnapping. Typical, let me be clear, in terms of cases I had defended in France. The job for me was to defend two different victims in two different cases. But when we met again, they showed me documents, and I began to investigate. I started to pull on a thread that, as it unraveled, brought me here today. [. . .] We realized that these were not isolated cases and that other people had had the same experiences as they did. The more we investigated, the more horrified we were by what we found. I can tell you now, because we have evidence, that an entire criminal organization was put in place, supported by the Franco regime, whose sole objective was to separate families in the

opposition from their own children. I am weighing my words, but I am talking about an actual, ideological mafia with an undercurrent not of ethnic cleansing but of political cleansing; I would even say their goal was to eliminate an entire social class. When you look at the hundreds of cases we have received, no other conclusion is possible. In each case, the victims were known to be anti-Franco militants or were families identified as having leftist politics. [. . .] But worst of all is that this trafficking of children continued after the demise of the Franco regime. We have cases that date from well after his death. I'm not at liberty to say more, because, as we heard live right here on your show, an inquiry has been opened, and I do not want to hinder the course of justice. But you have my word, we have proof. [. . .] So many people are impli-cated in this: public figures, the elite, the country's most influential families, as they say. People knew right up to the highest echelons of power, and no one said a thing. It has to end. It's time to speak out. Don't be afraid. Above all, what's most important is that the people who created this system or who profited from it pay for what they did."

Deeply troubled by Isabel's statement, Diego wanted to see for himself what she brought him. He was not disappointed. What he saw was absolutely staggering. A criminal, mafia-style organi-zation as sophisticated as it was corrupt. She has struck upon something enormous. From the very first, he had sensed that this was going to be out of the ordinary, but he never imagined to what extent. The statements and, above all, the official documents that Isabel has located, cover a period beginning in 1945 and ending in 2006. More than sixty years . . . He almost can't believe it.

He is also impressed by the lawyer and the job she pulled off. Timid and reserved at first, she slowly relaxed as the hours passed. They sat across the table from each other to record the interview but moved gradually closer over the course of the evening. Face-to-face at first, they were sitting side by side hours later, on two high stools at the bar. Under the combined effect of fatigue and alcohol (after a couple of coffees, they moved on to vodka and almost finished an entire bottle), they shared stories about themselves, or rather about their lives. Isabel told him about some of her most famous cases in Paris; Diego talked about some of his reporting in Latin America. Communicating in this way helped create a relationship of trust that they both needed. In a scandal of the sort they're facing, it's good to know you can rely on someone. Diego is not unmoved by their close physical proximity. He has not so much as brushed up against a female body for a long time. He didn't tell Isabel about Carolina, but he suspects she knows. Since Carolina's death, he has had neither the desire nor the occasion to sleep with a woman. However, there is something about Isabel that he can't put his finger on. She is very beautiful; that's clear. But it isn't just her beauty. She radiates both a strength and a sensuality that attracts him. Yet whenever they get too close to each other, he can see Carolina. And he immediately shies away.

It is daylight when they finally leave Casa Pepe. Isabel phoned Ana to let her know there was nothing to worry about and that she could get home on her own. Diego walks her to her car. The gray van is still parked a few yards away, waiting to follow. The two men seated inside look to be sleeping. And annoyed. With good reason: not long after the two women left the car last night, they got a call from their chief.

"Nice job, boys; you managed to blow your cover," he announced. "Don't worry. It so happens that I know the woman you saw with Isabel Ferrer. A word of warning: she's going to come by to see you in a little while. Just stay calm and be polite, do you hear me? I'll take care of the rest. Also, you'll give her what she asks for; that's an order. I'll deal with the consequences . . ."

Surprised by the call, they don't notice Ana walking toward them until they have hung up the phone. They remain in the van. The one at the wheel fiddles with his phone, the other lights a cigarette and squirms in his seat. The detective walks up to the passenger side of the van and taps at the window. They pretend not to notice. She knocks harder. They continue to stare straight ahead. Ana grabs the handle and yanks the door open.

"What's wrong, cat got your tongue?" she starts in on them. "Hey you, meathead! I'm talking to you! Are we going to have a nice little chat, or am I going to have to call up your chief again?"

They were expecting to see a woman but not one with a mouth on her like this. The two intelligence agents turn to look at her at exactly the same moment.

"What?" they say back in unison.

"Oh, so now you can talk! I just have one thing to tell you. I know you're obeying orders and all that, blah, blah, blah. Your orders were to keep Isabel Ferrer under surveillance. I can understand, given the shitload of trouble she's stirring up. But let me just give you a warning: if you ever hurt her, and I'm not saying you would, or if something ever happens to her, I promise you now that I will find you and take care of you. Capiche?"

"Who the hell are you? You think you can scare us?" the driver retorts dryly.

"You're taking this the wrong way. I'm just letting you know. Oh, and one last thing. The other day when she was attacked, you were there, right? And you didn't do anything? A couple of cowards, the both of you. That reminds me, your chief told me to tell you to hand over the photos you took at the scene. I hope you know how to use a camera at least."

Ana takes the SD card that one of the agents pushes at her and walks off without saying goodbye. She had to pull some strings to find out who put a tail on Isabel. When she learned it was the National Intelligence Center, she immediately phoned her contact there. He owed Ana a favor for the help she gave him on a counterespionage case, so it was easy. From about twenty feet away, she turns around and lets them know with a gesture that she's not done with them yet.

Knowing nothing about that encounter, which took place while they were recording the interview, Isabel and Diego are heading home, exhausted from staying up all night. Before getting into her car, the lawyer places a hand on the journalist's arm and brings her face close to his. She kisses him on the corner of his mouth, lets out a "thanks," and gets behind the wheel. Startled, Diego is still rooted to the spot when she turns the corner. As he steps to the curb, he is almost knocked over by a gray van that passes by him at full speed.

A dark figure hurries down the street. He walks furtively, hands in his pockets, a cap on his head and a black backpack on his shoulders. His face is barely visible, only lit briefly whenever he passes under a streetlamp. It is nearly midnight and time for his appointment. He darts a look behind him every once in a while to make sure no one is following, but he sees no one. Even at this relatively early hour in a neighborhood not far from downtown Madrid, few people are out and about. The truth is that at midweek, only tourists come here; the residents all prefer to stay home. No one has the cash to go out to the bars anymore or watch a League of Champions match, like tonight. Madrid's two main teams, Real and Atlético, have already been eliminated. And no self-respecting Madrileño would root for Barça, their longtime rival. In any case, ever since the financial crisis hit, fans can no longer treat themselves to stadium tickets or their favorite team's overpriced soccer jerseys, nor do they even care to pay attention to the temper tantrums of mere kids who are paid millions to run after a ball. "Bread and circuses," as the saying goes. In the case of the former, you first have to be able to make ends meet to fill your stomach. As for fun and games . . . some other time. Only the lottery offers any hope, as fantastical as it may be, of a better life, which is to say one where you can pay your rent on time and decently fill your fridge.

He is of average height with a muscular, athletic build that even his parka can't hide. He slows down when he arrives in front of a tall, modern building. The walls are beige, and crosses feature prominently on the large stained glass windows. Standing in front of the entrance, he looks left and right, clears his throat, and spits on the door of the headquarters of the Church of Scientology in Spain. He laughs, pleased with his little act of vandalism, which he repeats every time he comes this way, and then he continues on down the street.

He turns the corner and approaches a nearby office tower, dark except for the top floor. That's where they are waiting for him. That's where he will have to report on what he has seen and heard at the NASB. And where he will get his next set of instructions. He senses that things are moving fast now and that they are going to ask him to turn up the heat. He can't wait. He wants to do something real, something physical. He's tired of spending his days with his nose glued to a computer screen, typing code with people he hates, which is what he has been doing the last few weeks. He enjoyed flexing his muscles on the lawyer and the journalist, but those jobs were small, and he's had enough of pretending to be a volunteer computer programmer. He knows it's God's will. And that God chose him for this mission. And that even if he doesn't always like the work, he's going to have to stay tough and see it through. The Church is in danger, thanks to this gang of Commie infidels. He has to do everything he can to protect it. He feels like a warrior, or rather a crusader—a fighter on the front lines of a battle that is about to break wide open.

He presses the intercom, buzzing twice quickly, which is the code. No name is written above the red button, just two black letters on a red background: CC. By chance, the Crusaders for Christ have set up office only a few hundred feet from the Scientologists. This extreme right-wing group of several thousand followers emerged from a schism with Opus Dei a few years earlier. They are Catholic fanatics who believe that a new war of civilizations is going to engulf Spain. They are as terrified of the former Socialist government as they are convinced it was hoodwinking them. The impetus for the group's creation was same-sex marriage, which the Socialists legalized as soon as they were in power. The Crusaders of Christ's purpose now consists mainly in spreading their beliefs, but it has been tough going. Their former accomplices at Opus Dei have a tight grip on the media and the current government—a situation that is pushing the group to radicalize and become more violent. Threatening statements have given way to hard-line actions at mosques, synagogues, and associations promoting HIV/AIDS awareness. They've thrown rocks and Molotov cocktails and beat people up. They even set fire to a warehouse belonging to an NGO working for the Red Cross.

He enters and takes the elevator to the top floor. The doors open onto a long, thickly carpeted corridor. The offices that line it are empty at this late hour. All their doors are closed. At the end of the hallway, a light shines from under one door: they are already here. He walks quickly toward it and enters what appears to be a conference room. A group of men is seated around a large, oval table. Some wear dark suits and ties, others clerical vestments. The priests are dressed uniformly in black cassocks. One individual, who is seated regally at the head of the table, stands out from this monochrome assembly: draped in the red-and-black robes of a cardinal in the Catholic Church, he looks for all the world as if he has just arrived from the Roman Curia of the Vatican. He invites the man to take a seat with a simple gesture of one hand, on which he wears a large gold signet ring.

"Good evening, my son. Sit down and tell us everything you know. When you have finished, we will tell you what to do next. So far, you have conducted yourself very well, and I'm sure you will continue to do so and that you won't disappoint us."

13

THE DECISION CAME down exactly as he expected. David Ponce has been dismissed from the magistrature. He wasn't fired exactly, but he was suspended without pay. However, only until his dismissal is formalized. The disciplinary board took just a few minutes to pronounce a judgment. But Ponce made it easy for them, refusing to answer questions and offering nothing in his defense. What difference would it have made? Their minds had already been made up by the powers that be, and he had no intention of discussing anything with them. The only thing that surprised him was their spinelessness: he expected to be fired, but instead, he was punished, like a child. A provisional sanction until a trial can be held and a verdict delivered on charges of abuse of power and wrongdoing. If Ponce is found guilty, he will be removed definitively. If he is acquitted, he'll be transferred as far from Madrid as they can send him, most likely some jurisdiction in the sticks. But he is dead sure of how this is going to go down. He'll be tried and found guilty. For attempting to circumvent the Amnesty Law: guilty. For wanting to expose the worst of the dictatorship: guilty. For inconveniencing the country's most powerful people: guilty. For fighting for justice: guilty. For asking the country to examine its past, to show some courage, to dig into its collective memory, and to settle the score with history once and for all: guilty on all counts. Special proceedings have been invoked. The hearing will take place imminently. It couldn't be soon enough for him. In a few weeks, a ruling will be made, and he will be free.

After Ponce's drive-through appearance before the disciplinary board, its twelve members asked him to leave the room and wait in the corridor, like a common defendant summoned before a judge. All the same, it was strange to have the shoe on the other foot. He knew what he risked by coming alone, without counsel, and what they were plotting for him. He used the time to call Diego and let him know how it was going.

"I'm dead meat," Ponce concluded, summing up the morning's events. "Isabel Ferrer is going to have to stick it out, even if I'm removed from the case. They'll have to appoint a replacement, but that's only to give the appearance of following procedure. From now on, we have to take the fight to the streets and the media. When are you going back on the air?"

"Damn, how are you taking it? Listen, if there's anything I can do . . . Wait, I have an idea. Why don't you come on the show, in the studio? Not a bad move, don't you think? I'm expecting to go back on this Friday. You could respond to Isabel's interview, live. She is more than ready for this, don't worry about that. I think she understands exactly what needs to be done to prevent this scandal from being brushed under the rug."

It's decided. With the magistrate live in the studio, Diego is going to go back on the air with guns blazing. The suspense will be intensified by the fact that, in the meantime, Ponce plans to avoid the hordes of cameras and microphones that are waiting for him to leave the hearing. Instead, he takes a side door normally reserved for high-profile figures appearing in court who would rather not see their problems with the justice system plastered on the front page of every paper. To exit this way requires going into the basement and taking a long corridor that follows the path of the building's wastewater pipes, then coming out onto a small side street that runs parallel to the courthouse. No, he's not going to give the press anything, not now. He'll save his first public statement for Diego's show. But that's not all; before hanging up, the two friends agreed on a little surprise for Diego's listeners: an announcement that will set tongues wagging in the hallways of the courthouse. The journalist would have liked to have Isabel as a guest on his show, too, along with the judge, but she declined his invitation. No need for her to be there, she made it clear to him: Diego already has the interview that he wanted. Which is true. But he would have liked to see her again.

In the meantime, Diego has an appointment with Ana. She found something. Also, she has pictures to show him. The detective didn't say much more than that on the phone, but he could tell from the tone of her voice that she has something big. In no time, he is rapping on the window of her agency. Her office is located on the ground floor of a small building. Her apartment is above it, on the first floor, and the two spaces are linked by a spiral staircase. She doesn't draw much of a distinction between her private life and her professional life. Like Diego, she lives for her work. It's what gets her out of bed in the morning, and it's what keeps her going. Whether Ana likes it or not, her imprisonment during the years of the dictatorship in Argentina and the brutal interrogations she endured at the hands of the secret police have left deep scars. The kind you don't see. The kind that haunt you. The kind that wake you up in the middle of the night screaming. Not only was she working within a clandestine organization to overthrow the generals in power, but she had only just begun to transition to a woman. This incited her torturers to abuse her even more atrociously. She wasn't exactly a man then, but she wasn't fully a woman either. The bastards went crazy on her. She still has nightmares, thirty years later. She never tires of telling Diego: "If I ever find the guy who did that to me, I swear I'll kill him with my bare hands." He believes her. He knows Ana's capable of it.

For the moment, it's the middle of the day. She opens the door and invites the journalist to talk upstairs. "We'll have more privacy up there, and we'll be more comfortable," she explains, locking the front door and pulling the blinds over the windows of the agency. In the apartment, she starts by bringing up the photos on her computer taken by the intelligence agents of Isabel's attack. Diego is surprised at first that Ana could get her hands on these, but he bursts into laughter when he hears the story of how she did. He squints, moves closer to the screen, and looks at them one after the other. His gaze is drawn first to the terrified expression on the lawyer's face. He feels a tightness in his chest and a lump in his throat. Something else he sees makes him look closer. He zooms in, but the photo quality is mediocre, and when the picture breaks into pixels, he can't make out what it is he thought he saw. Still, he's almost certain: it is the same man who attacked him.

"Yep, it's the same guy who punched me the other day."

"Are you sure?"

"Not one hundred percent, but look at that, there, around his neck. It looks like a red cross, like the one my attacker was wearing. And he has the same build. Yeah, I'd say it's him."

"Well, that's one thing we've settled. The real question is who this guy is, and who is giving him orders. I'm going to call my contact at the CNI to find out if he can trace him. In the meantime, look at this."

Ana walks around to the other side of the coffee table where she placed her computer and hands him two envelopes stuffed with papers.

"What's this?" Diego asks.

"I told you that I thought I had seen the name of that nun somewhere. Well, I went through all my files and, if you can believe it, I found her. Don't get up; you won't believe it."

"What? Go on, tell me!"

"I found her name on papers relating to that notary, Pedro De La Vega. The one that Isabel hired me to investigate."

"What?"

"You see? I told you!" says Ana excitedly.

"How? What's the connection?"

"Well, if you can believe it, she worked in a maternity ward in Madrid when she was young. We're talking in the forties and fifties. That was also when the notary was just opening his practice. As he was just starting out, he took on a lot of insignificant work, not like later, if you see what I mean. Real estate transactions. Registering small businesses. And adoptions. He even developed quite a specialty in those."

"I'm not following . . ."

"Wait, let me finish! He legalized about a hundred adoptions for couples in a single year, 1946. And in a lot of these papers he prepared for the court, who is the character witness for the adopting families? A certain Sister Marie-Carmen . . . The dear old nun! Isn't that the greatest?"

Diego is speechless, stunned by what Ana has just told him. He tries to recover from the shock, but it's a struggle. His mind is racing. It is too much to process. He needs a minute to absorb what the detective has discovered. In the time it takes to drink the coffee she made him, the motor starts up again. The engine roars back to life. The brain cells begin firing again. Thanks to Ana, he has a new angle on the case. A notary and a nun, both murdered in two different cities, several months apart. They were killed in almost identical ways, by a single bullet to the head, fired at close range. A notary and a nun who knew each other or who, at the very least, had been in contact years earlier. A notary and a nun whose names appear on adoption papers completed during the dictatorship. It's no coincidence.

Diego decides to start over from the beginning. First, the notary's murder. He also needs to find out more about the death of Sister Marie-Carmen. But he can't do everything at once. He has to prepare his show with David Ponce and the interview with Isabel Ferrer. Then, he'll look into De La Vega and try to get access to the files on both murders. Then . . . Well, he'll see what he knows then. He and Ana agree to wait a few days before getting started. They each have a job to finish. Everything in due time. Patience and reflection are both key to this kind of work. No need to rush. In principle, they are the only ones who have established a link between the two victims. They're well ahead of the media, who don't give a damn about the death of an old notary and a wrinkled, elderly nun, even in such violent circumstances, when a national scandal is threatening to shake the country to its very core.

Diego has received confirmation that he can go back on the air. When he told Radio Uno's directors that the next show would include not only an interview with Isabel Ferrer but also a special appearance by David Ponce, they released the news immediately. Everyone has been talking about it since Friday morning. Even though the journalist refused to build up the suspense by making any hints about the content of the show, which infuriated the station's communications director, the news dropped like a bombshell. The next episode of *Radio Confidential* is so highly anticipated that many station employees are foregoing Friday night plans to stick around until the show airs. Everyone wants to watch the show live. Diego could not be more exasperated. For someone who records his show every week in the isolation of the basement studio at a time when the station is practically deserted, the number of people who are still sitting in their offices or making their way toward the studio is starting to get on his nerves. When he sees Radio Uno's president and most of its executive board, followed by several cameramen, squeezing into the tiny control booth while the producer tries to make room for them all, his temper explodes. He's on in less than fifteen minutes, but the only thing he knows right now is that he will not do the show in front of a "studio audience."

"Out! Out!" he yells at his bosses. "Everybody out! What the hell is going on here? If you stay where you are, I'm not doing the show. Is that clear? Jesus, I can't believe it . . . Now! Clear out! I don't get it: one day you suspend me, and the next, every pooh-bah at the station wants to hang out with me. This isn't the circus here, and I don't make a habit of broadcasting for an audience. I'm warning you: I'm going to leave now to meet my guest and smoke a cigarette. If you're still here when I get back, I'm going home!"

Diego leaves, carrying his files under one arm and a cigarette already hanging from his lips, cursing the station directors. He has no idea how they will react. But he meant what he said—if they want him to do the show, they're going to have to get the hell out of the studio. He'd rather shoot himself in the foot than play their game. He's just finishing his cigarette when David Ponce appears out of nowhere. Diego explains the situation to him. The judge laughs and guarantees there will be nobody left in the studio when he goes back in. The station directors aren't that stupid. David's right; you can almost hear a pin drop in the studio when they arrive. The producer can't believe Diego's ruse worked, but everyone started to leave almost as soon as Diego took the elevator back upstairs. The producer heard they were moving to the boardroom and would listen to the show together there. They were disappointed to learn there would be no video feed. But Studio 4 is the only broadcast studio at Radio Uno that is not equipped with webcams or video cameras. Which is why Diego prefers it. Whoever thought of filming a radio show? It's what's done now, it's what people want, it's Radio 2.0, radio that connects with people, they all say. It's all bullshit, as far as Diego's concerned. He wanted to go into radio precisely because he wouldn't have to show his face. And now they want to put a camera in every studio.

The journalist and the judge take their places. There is just enough time to do a quick sound check before the show launches. Headphones on, Diego greets his listeners with his usual, "Good evening, night prowlers," and announces the program for this special edition. David Ponce watches him go through his paces. He appreciates the journalist's professionalism and admires Diego's poise and easy banter. He fiddles with his lighter and smiles when his host signals to him to get ready for his interview but that he has time for a quick smoke if he wants, all the while speaking into the microphone as if nothing else was going on. He has exactly three minutes, while Prosecutor X's segment airs. A rerun tonight. With everything happening, there was no time to prepare a new one.

"So before we get started, how should I address you tonight? Your honor? Mister Ponce? David Ponce?" Diego begins.

"David is fine, thanks. We're not going to pretend anymore that we don't know each other. As for my professional title, for the moment, I am still a judge, but I don't know for how long."

"How do you feel about that?"

"Listen, I'll be honest. I won't say I'm not upset. But I'm not particularly surprised. When I called into your show to announce I would be opening an inquiry into this story of babies kidnapped under the Franco regime, I knew what the risks were. I would do the same thing again."

Diego questions David for the next twenty minutes. The judge makes a good impression. He doesn't want to be the victim here. His goal is for everyone to understand that the National Association of Stolen Babies has very valid reasons for existing. That justice must be delivered. That it's time the people responsible for this odious crime are made to pay for it.

"One last question, David, if you don't mind. It's along the same lines as the one I asked you at the start of this interview. I'll admit I already know the answer, but, for my listeners, I have to ask it, and I know that everyone listening is in for quite a surprise. . . . So I'll just go ahead. David, are you Prosecutor X?"

"I've been unmasked!" David Ponce jokes. "Yes, that's me."

"There you have it, listeners; yet another revelation tonight. The true identity of our famous Prosecutor X, anonymous no longer. I hope that, beginning next week, David will return to regale us with his mordant observations, in plain view this time."

A musical break follows so that everyone—the producer, David, and Diego at his microphone—can catch their breath before continuing. Isabel Ferrer's interview is up next, and it promises to create an even bigger sensation. Diego insists on choosing the music for every show himself. Between two and three songs, depending on the week. Always reflecting the content of the show in some way. For tonight, he chose a song that everyone in Spain knows by heart, the 1974 hit "Porque te vas" (Because you are leaving), sung by Jeanette: an obvious nod to Judge Ponce's imminent dismissal from the magistrature. A doubly significant choice because it was the theme song of Carlos Saura's 1976 film *Cría Cuervos*, not only an allegorical tale of death and the loss of a loved one, but also about the complicated relationships between children and adults, namely between the members of a rigid bourgeois family entangled in the morals and codes of Francoist Spain. Upstairs, in Radio Uno's boardroom, no one is listening to Diego's musical selections. The station directors are trying to look like they didn't just learn the identity of Prosecutor X, live on the show like everyone else. Whispered conversations circle the table. The question on everyone's lips is whether to keep this rather bothersome but cheap chronicler

(David has never asked to be paid for his information) or forbid him from coming back on the air, effective as of the next show.

In the studio, Diego and David are enjoying the fuss they've created. The judge plans to stay to listen to Isabel's interview and respond to it on the air. The recording hasn't even started to run, and already the show is an overwhelming success. The audience must be huge, judging from the number of calls coming in on the switchboard. For the first time in the history of *Radio Confidential*, Diego will run a full hour of the interview, much longer than he has ever done. The context, the interviewee, and the content persuaded him he didn't have any other choice. The fact that he didn't have enough time to edit it into a tighter format also had something to do with it.

"People knew right up to the highest echelons of power, and no one said a thing."

Isabel's statement closes the interview with the finality of a guillotine blade. Ten seconds of silence, an eternity, add the final punctuation mark. Diego is a master of suspense and knows how to manipulate the codes of radio broadcasting to his advantage. He can wield a microphone like others would a sword. A razor-sharp one. David Ponce says only that he would rather let the lawyer's words speak for themselves, praising Isabel's courage and wishing her and the NASB the best of luck in their fight. Closing credits. Tune in next week. For a return to more standard fare. Or not . . .

A strong smell of paint hits Isabel as she enters her building. Despite her exhaustion after staying up all night with Diego, she has only been home to change clothes before returning to the NASB's offices. The staff has been gripped by paranoia ever since the meeting with Ana, and Isabel needed to calm her team down. Ana has not finished checking the backgrounds of the volunteers, but nothing has turned up yet. Isabel is troubled too by the way she said goodbye to the journalist. When she kissed Diego, it seemed like the natural thing to do; still, she doesn't understand why she did it. It's not that Isabel doesn't find him attractive, quite the contrary, but she wonders what it could lead to. To take her mind off it, she has thrown herself into her work even more than usual. She has gathered so many documents, photos, and stacks of papers that it will take an obsessive attention to detail to make sense of it all. Lost in her thoughts, Isabel doesn't notice that several of her neighbors are gathered at the foot of the staircase. They are speaking to her in loud voices and trying to get her attention. She jumps when she finally sees them. Some look angry, and some look worried. They have been waiting for her. The president of the building's co-op board silences everyone with a gesture. The woman begins explaining to Isabel what has happened. Without hearing the president out, she runs up the stairs to the second floor. Out of breath, she stops dead in her tracks in front of her apartment door, petrified. The strong odor in the building is coming from here. Her door has been splattered with red paint to resemble blood stains, and there is a note whose meaning leaves no doubt as to the vandals' intentions: *"You are Satan. You will burn in Hell."*

The attacker who found her in the street has now made it to her door. The threats are more violent and have crossed from the public realm into the private one. Clearly, she is no longer safe at home. The first thing she does is take photos of the door from as many angles as possible. Isabel disturbs none of the evidence and calls Ana, even though her first instinct is to phone Diego, to hear the sound of his voice. But she needs to keep her head on her shoulders. The private detective will know how to advise her on what to do. Isabel refuses to listen to her neighbors, who are insisting she call the police. She would really rather not. There's no guarantee they would even investigate properly, aware of what everyone knows about her now. In fact, the opposite would more likely be true. And what if this was a government-ordered job? Moreover, letting the cops into her apartment would not be a good idea. The last thing she needs is a police search that would turn up her weapons and the files on her victims, which would create an even more embarrassing situation.

When Ana arrives, she finds Isabel sitting on the stairs, head in her hands, alone and dozing. Isabel's exhaustion has finally caught up with her. Ana takes one look at the door and makes a phone call, then wakes Isabel gently and the two women enter the apartment. A brief look around confirms there was not a break-in as well. Isabel collapses onto the couch while Ana pours her a glass of wine. Something to get her spirits back up and help her think through the next few days. The detective suggests she come stay with her until things calm down, which she accepts gratefully.

"And there's something else I need to tell you," Ana continues. "Have you noticed a gray delivery van parked outside your building?"

"No. To be honest, I haven't paid much attention."

"Well, let me explain. You've been under surveillance by the CNI, you know, the National Intelligence Center."

"You're joking!" Isabel says, shocked.

"The only thing that would surprise me is if that wasn't the case. At least it proves the CNI is doing their job. I know one of the directors there. I called him as soon as I got here and saw what happened. The two agents assigned to your case are going to come up here and take a good look at your door. Then, you're going to go with them. They want to talk to you."

"Go with them? Where? I thought I was going to your place."

"They just want to go over some things with you," says Ana, reassuringly. "My contact wouldn't say anything else. But don't worry. I guarantee you, he's on our side. When you're done, I'll come get you, and tonight, we can have a girls' dinner, just the two of us."

By the time Isabel has put together an overnight bag, the two agents have arrived to meet their suspect in person for the first time. Back in the street a few moments later, Isabel is about to get into the gray van when her phone rings. It's a call from France. Her mother. With the news that her grandmother has just been taken to the hospital in critical condition.

14

IT GOES WITHOUT saying that Diego's interview with Isabel was the top story of the weekend. All the print and broadcast media and Internet news sites launched an avalanche of special editions, reports, and debates, some more serious than others and featuring professionals from every imaginable field. Or really anyone with a title who loves to be invited on set and whom television loves to put in the spotlight as soon as an occasion presents itself. Pseudo-criminologists, psychiatrists with credentials from universities no one has ever heard of, obscure constitutional scholars, and researchers who have never discovered anything in their lives. Quite simply, "experts" full of hot air who like to listen to themselves talk or throw out banalities wrapped up in savant discourse. The usual pundits, always ready to pick a fight on camera, knowing that the media, audiences, and the companies selling ad time couldn't be happier, allowing a thirty-second publicity spot to sell for a fortune. A deplorable spectacle that sucks up all the oxygen and airtime so that the real issues can't be discussed. Talk shows that have the blessing of the government, which much prefers that the country amuse itself, even with serious issues, rather than actually think.

In that department, the hands-down champions are the privately owned stations. But not long after the APM was elected, the public services followed suit. No one was surprised: the new minister of culture and communication was previously the director of the leading private TV station in the country. He resigned to take over the ministry, whose purpose seems to be to quash any unfavorable publicity and to grant favors to friends. Most importantly, his friends, his colleagues' friends, friends of deputies and senators, and basically everyone who worked in the wings (by financing the APM's campaign) to win the elections. In just the first week on the job, the minister appointed his cronies to lead the major public media outlets in a frenzy of Berlusconism. Luckily, there are a few resisters left like Diego, and he's not alone. Several websites, available only to paying subscribers, have popped up, created by seasoned journalists who lost their jobs at the main media conglomerates due to the shake-up. All are critical, extremely critical even, of the state of affairs in the country and the austerity measures implemented to try to resolve it. The economic crisis hit the media particularly hard. Most of the national dailies have made drastic cuts to their workforces, and they all look alike now: less and less investigative reporting, and more and more of everything that is trivial or supposed to be clever or buzzworthy. If all the news shows on all the stations, public and private, were watched side by side, you would think their content was chosen for them at Moncloa, the prime minister's residence. Just like when Franco was in power.

At the moment, however, Diego's mind is elsewhere. His focus now is on the files that Isabel gave him. His goal is to make headway by rereading them in the light of Ana's revelations concerning the notary public and the nun. Experience and intuition tell him that both murders are connected to the scandal of the stolen babies. Diego doesn't have any proof yet; he's not sure how or why, but as far as he can tell, it is the most likely hypothesis. These latest developments have only confirmed what he could scarcely imagine when he first saw the documents that were left outside his apartment with the plane ticket for Paris. One of those documents was an adoption certificate signed by Pedro De La Vega. Still, many questions remain, and Diego won't rest until he gets some answers. His next show is scheduled in two weeks, due to a public holiday that falls on the following Friday, but that doesn't leave him much time.

Radio Uno's directors are exasperated. First, they had to wait to discover the identity of Prosecutor X along with the rest of the country. Second, they consented to Diego's demand to evacuate Studio 4, effectively exiling them to the boardroom to listen to the show. And after all that, they had no other choice but to congratulate the journalist. His editorial one-two punch—two exclusive interviews: Isabel Ferrer's about the creation of the National Association of Stolen Babies, followed by the immediate reaction of the future ex-judge David Ponce—has been the only thing anyone has talked about for the last forty-eight hours. What else could they do? Radio Uno has been getting free publicity and was served the perfect opportunity to shore up its reputation and vaunt its editorial independence from the government, as relative as that may be.

Diego's living room looks like a document archive. Papers are strewn everywhere: on the table, on the floor, on the couch, and even on the counters of his open-plan kitchen. He has taped photos to his walls—mostly old pictures in black and white—and wherever there was any space remaining, he has pasted Post-its. Anyone walking in would declare it a disaster area, but for the journalist, there is a method to his madness. Every document occupies a precise location, and every Post-it indicates a question. On one side of the apartment are the papers Isabel gave him, in chronological order. On the other side is Ana's report on the notary, Pedro De La Vega, along with the statements of the Valencia police officers and the autopsy report on Sister Marie-Carmen, which he was able to get his hands on through a contact who was once one of his sources within the Madrid Police Department but who was transferred to Valencia a few years ago. Stacked in a corner are dozens of photocopies of books from his visits to the library. He has been pacing the apartment for a while, a coffee in one hand and a cigarette burning into an overflowing ashtray, studying photos, rereading a passage of Ana's report or an extract of a certificate signed by the notary, comparing dates, and looking for what could tie it all together. Diego opens the window to get some air and turns up the volume on the stereo, which is playing "Nights in the

Gardens of Spain" by Manuel de Falla, his favorite composer. Then he returns to the living room. Then he takes another look at the photos. Then he rereads another passage from the documents. Diego is worn out and feeling overwhelmed by the scope of it all. He is just lighting another cigarette when an idea comes to him. He closes the window, turns off the music, and begins looking for his recording of the interview with Emilia Ferrer on his computer. He puts on his headphones and presses "Play" while looking over the notes he took during the afternoon he spent with the lawyer's grandmother. It only takes him three minutes to find what his subconscious had already picked up on. It was right there under his nose, or rather in his ears, so close he can't believe he didn't see it before. "What an idiot I am!" he scolds himself.

There's no time for gloating over his find, though. The intercom buzzes. It's Ana, who is out of breath.

"Open up! I have to talk to you!"

She rushes past him into the apartment without a word of greeting.

"Hi to you too," Diego tosses back at her, but his curiosity is piqued.

Rarely has he observed his friend in such a state of excitement. Looking for somewhere to sit and seeing that every inch of space is covered, Ana remains standing and announces in a loud voice that she knows the NASB was infiltrated. She knows who did it and that it was the same man who attacked Diego and Isabel, and that he is a member of the Crusaders for Christ, which her contact at the CNI confirmed.

"Wow, that was unexpected! How did you figure that out?"

Ana gets ready to explain, opens her mouth, and then changes her mind.

"Wait, before I tell you, I've got one . . . no, two other pieces of news. The first is that Isabel has gone with the CNI. They were tailing her for a while, and they want to talk to her because the threats on her life are getting more serious. The second is that she's going to have to leave for Paris. Her grandmother has been hospitalized in critical condition. She had a heart attack."

"Shit! I hope Emilia's going to make it. Really, the CNI is on this? I guess that was to be expected. Is it your friend, at least? I'm guessing it is, or you wouldn't have let her go with them."

"Yeah, it's his unit, fortunately," says Ana. "I can trust him; there won't be any dirty tricks. He's an agent, but he's a good guy."

"And a mostly honest one, though I'm not sure you can say that about someone whose job it is to spy on his fellow citizens."

"Stop it; we're not going to have an argument about him again. You know we need guys like him to do his job. Let me remind you that without him, the terrorist attacks of 2004 would never have been solved, and we'd still be saying it was the ETA behind them and not Al-Qaeda."

"I'll grant you that. Well, go ahead, tell me the rest."

She gives him a full report in just a few minutes. She explains that her investigation into the association's volunteers didn't turn up anything, but a certain number of names were missing from the files. So she decided to go to the NASB's headquarters to get the names of its newest members and anyone else who had recently offered to help without joining. She was talking to a few people from the executive committee, and they told her that the atmosphere had started to go downhill after they began to receive the anonymous letters. So she took a walk around the office, just to scope things out, talk to whoever was there, and to pick up some of the conversations. There were a lot of people because of the march being planned in Madrid in a few days. They were painting banners and creating flyers. They were excited. After waiting for this moment for so long, everyone was hopeful that thousands of people would respond to the call that went out on social media and the Internet; everyone wants to believe that this is going to get their movement off the ground and that the government will have to make gestures toward them. The bigger the crowds, the greater the pressure.

Just as she was getting ready to leave, she decided to take a look in the room where the IT team was set up. One of them stood out to her: he had his eyes glued to his screen and didn't seem to be taking part in the conversations going on around him. She stayed a minute to watch him. He was dressed in black. She came closer; he looked up at her and smiled. She couldn't believe it. It was the guy in the surveillance photos. To hide her surprise, she started chatting with him, asking him how things were going, how long he'd been with the association. Just an ordinary conversation. His voice was kind of high. And when he leaned forward to hook up a hard drive to his computer, she saw it: a chain around his neck, and a red cross. The same one that was visible in the agents' photos. *Bingo!* She left without saying a word to anyone and called her contact at the CNI. He told Ana the IT worker's name and about his involvement with the Crusaders for Christ. And that the CNI had identified him only a few days earlier because the worker doesn't have a criminal record, but they didn't put a tail on him because the CNI couldn't spare any more resources. These ultra-conservative Catholic organizations are not on the terrorist watch list, so they aren't considered a security threat, and no one wants to throw money at putting surveillance on them. So said the orders from the top. Of course, the fact that the director of the CNI is an eminent member of Opus Dei did not influence that decision in any way whatsoever . . .

"You mean, it's just a coincidence that these wackos aren't considered dangerous for the country's security . . . Incredible!" Diego lets his temper fly.

"Take it easy! The CNI might not be able to do anything, but my contact and I came up with an idea: we can trap him. And it will be only too fun to use a tried-and-true method. Some good old-fashioned blackmail."

Isabel landed in Paris only a few hours after getting her mother's phone call and being taken to the CNI headquarters. Now she is back in France, after eighteen months of exile in Spain, all of which flew past in a kind of fever dream. The fatigue and tension of the past several weeks overwhelm her all at once. She is on edge, not so much because of her questioning at the National

Intelligence Center but because of her grandmother's health. Isabel still doesn't know exactly what happened to Emilia or what her condition is. She just hopes it's not too serious. But Isabel is sure that if her family asked her to come back immediately, she should expect the worst.

They didn't keep her long at the CNI, given the news from Paris. Nevertheless, she waited a while in a windowless room on the basement level of the agency's headquarters, in an ordinary looking building on Madrid's main avenue, the Gran Via. When the two agents assigned to her case brought her there, she started to panic.

"Is this an official questioning?" she asked, her mounting fear creeping into her voice.

"No, don't worry," one of the cops reassured her. "Our chief is on his way. He just wants to talk to you."

Ten, fifteen, twenty, thirty minutes passed. It seemed like an endless wait. Isabel stayed seated the whole time. With sweaty hands, she tried to download her email on her smartphone. A waste of time. No network connection. Finally, a man walked in without knocking. He was of average height and used a cane to walk, and his movement was slow because of a limp. He looked tired and old beyond his years; he was probably only sixty, if that. He was bald and thin-lipped with blue eyes and a graying goatee. He had a deep baritone voice that was surprising coming from his slight frame. He was carrying a file under one arm and extended the other hand to Isabel as he approached her, but she did not take it. He didn't seem to notice.

"Hello, my name is Nicolás Ortiz. I apologize for the wait and this impromptu meeting in such dreary surroundings. I want to start by reassuring you that you have nothing to fear; I'm an old friend of Ana Durán's. I'm sorry to learn about your grandmother. I'm not going to keep you long so you can leave to join her as quickly as possible. My agents can take you home and then to the airport if you'd like. But I wanted to see you to discuss these threats you have been receiving. They are becoming more insistent and sufficiently explicit for us to take them very seriously."

"Is that why you have had me under surveillance? To protect me? Or to report my every movement and activity to your superiors, who will send it up the line, right to the government?"

Ortiz smiled. He was expecting her to say as much. Despite her anxiousness, Isabel couldn't contain her anger.

"Ana warned me you had spunk, and you're making an excellent display of it. I can understand your frustration, but let me just explain something: I do not work for the politicians running this country, and neither do my men. We serve our country and our fellow citizens. Everyone, and without exception. Yes, you were under surveillance. Can we agree it was a routine measure? One day you appear out of nowhere, and in the space of a single press conference, you unleash a shit storm, pardon the expression. But not all of us at the CNI are filthy fascists, or Franco throwbacks, or APM militants. On the contrary. We are the guardians of our democracy. That might sound pompous to you, but it's the truth. Just ask anyone; Ana, for example, will tell you about me.

She'll confirm for you that my nickname in this honorable institution is *El Rojo*, the Red. I'll leave it up to you to find out why."

After these introductions, Ortiz showed Isabel some of the evidence his agents had gathered during their investigation, as well as biometric photos of her assailant, but she was unable to identify the man in the photos as her attacker. She was more worried to discover that an organization that went by the name of Crusaders for Christ even existed and that it wanted to silence her. She had heard plenty of rumors about Opus Dei but was shocked to learn that a violent group of ultra-traditionalists in its midst had provoked a schism.

They were not her priority just now, however. Isabel's immediate task was to get to her grandmother's bedside as quickly as possible. She rushed from her plane into a taxi as fast as she could. She refused to cry during the drive to the Bichat Hospital in her grandmother's neighborhood. When she arrived, she got lost in the huge hospital complex, wasting precious time running from floor to floor before finally finding her grandmother's room. The corridor is deserted and strangely quiet. She knocks on the door but enters without waiting for a reply. Her grandmother is lying in the bed with her eyes closed, her head elevated and supported on either side by two pillows. Her complexion is pale, almost gray. She is motionless and appears to be sleeping. Isabel's mother is seated next to the bedside and has obviously been crying. When she sees Isabel, she rises and comes forward to take her daughter in her arms.

"It's over," she murmurs in her ear. "It's over. Grandma is gone. She is at peace now."

"Oh, Grandma, no!"

The tears start flowing, and Isabel is powerless to control it, to stop them, to move, to take a step toward Emilia's body to place a kiss on her forehead, as she always did, one last time.

Isabel is in shock. She can't remember anything about the two days that follow her arrival in Paris, as if they didn't happen, as if time had stopped until the funeral. It was there, at the Montmartre Cemetery, in the plot her grandparents purchased so long ago shortly after they came to France in the early 1950s, that Emilia was laid to rest next to her husband. And where the loss of her grandmother finally hits Isabel. An enormous emptiness interrupted only by intermittent thoughts of Diego. She is surprised to find herself wishing he was there at her side. The ceremony is brief, intimate, and emotional. As soon as it is over, Isabel decides to go to her grandmother's apartment on Rue Lamarck one last time. She spent a large part of her childhood there. Isabel wants to look one last time at the place where her grandparents practically raised her, where she grew so close to Emilia. Hours of playtime, talking, and reading books together. Experiences that made her the woman she is today, influenced by this grandmother whom she worshipped more than anyone else, who taught her to read and write and passed on everything she knew while giving Isabel the freedom to make her own decisions. She wants a few souvenirs, but there are so many! She takes some old photos. Then she shuts the door behind her for good. It's time to return to Madrid. Staying in France even one more day is out of the question. Too emotional. Too much work waiting for her in Spain. Too much happening at once.

At precisely the same time that Isabel is burying her grandmother, the demonstration organized by the National Association of Stolen Babies begins. The crowd is enormous, packed in behind a white banner bearing a single word in capital letters: JUSTICIA. The NASB's executive committee leads the procession. Behind them, thousands, perhaps tens of thousands, of people march in silence. Entire families—men and women, the old and the young—have answered the association's call. A turnout so huge it has surpassed the organizers' expectations. So much so the police can barely contain the crowd. As always, the official numbers are hotly disputed: 50,000 according to the police, but 150,000 according to the NASB. Some of the marchers carry photos; others brandish homemade signs sending poignant messages: SEARCHING FOR MY TWINS, BORN MAY 1973, MADRID; HELP ME FIND MY DAUGHTER, BORN AUGUST 1982, VALENCIA. Some are more direct: YOU BOUGHT MY SON . . . NOW GIVE HIM BACK! Others demand answers: WHERE ARE THE STOLEN BABIES? A woman in her sixties wears a wedding dress and holds a doll, the face of which has been covered by a large question mark. Around her neck, the woman wears a cardboard sign bearing a date, a tiny drawing of a child's head, and a question:

APRIL 5, 1976 . . . WHERE ARE YOU, MY DARLING?
Beyond the marchers' legitimate demands for justice, the most
common and moving sight is the mothers holding MISSING
posters high over their heads. For the first time, they are showing
themselves and speaking out, accusing the Church, the politicians, and the doctors of participating in the kidnappings and
profiting financially from them with total impunity.

When the first wave of marchers arrives in complete silence
at the Puerta del Sol, thousands are still waiting to leave the starting point, not far from the Buen Retiro Park. There will not be
room for everyone at the finish. As they keep arriving, the square
can no longer contain them all, and the adjacent pedestrian
streets are soon overrun with marchers. Then the first applause is
heard. Eventually, everyone begins to clap. For five full minutes,
Madrid's downtown rolls with the thunder of thousands of hands
clapping, as loud as any percussion concert.

The police are on high alert. Anti-riot units are stationed along
the entire length of the route, and the intelligence services are
moving through the crowd or have taken position on the balco-
nies of City Hall or on apartment buildings overlooking the
demonstration, where they film everything. Their job is to prevent the rally from degenerating at the hands of vandals and
right-wing extremists or anyone who would like to make trouble.
The risk is real. The fascist fringes have called on their militants
to attack these "anti-patriotic" marchers, these "Commies" and
"traitors." The inevitable happens when, two hours later, as the
crowds are dispersing and people are heading home, a group of

about thirty thugs shows up. They wear ski masks and wield iron bars or carry motorcycle helmets slung across their chests. They begin by sacking the two newspaper stands in the center of the square as the crowd boos them. A small number of demonstrators try to intervene. The police are on the scene relatively quickly and quell the violence before it can spread. There are some clashes with the police, and tear gas is sprayed as a few people are arrested.

These scuffles cannot detract from the success of the demonstration, however. The NASB's gamble paid off with an enormous show of strength. Except for the agitators who arrived at the end, the march went off calmly. And with dignity, too. No one chanted. No one exchanged insults. A single statement was read by the NASB to a sea of cameras and microphones. The news stations carried it live. The foreign press was there as well, dispatching their local correspondents or even sending reporters just to cover it. The footage has been playing on a loop for hours. Artists came from all over to participate, and those who were unable to posted messages of support on their websites, Facebook pages, and Twitter feeds. The government will have no choice but to do something. Or rather, they will have to react. It cannot remain silent. It cannot do nothing. And for that reason alone, under pressure, it will recognize that there is, in fact, a problem and that something is rotten in the state of Spain. The government will try to play it down and consign it to the Franco era, another time, another place, and other customs. But it's likely that will not be enough.

15

NOTHING LIKE THIS has happened to Diego for a very long time. He's stuck. He has gone over what he knows a hundred or two hundred times in his head. Checked and reread the documents and listened again to the interview with Emilia Ferrer. Only one possible conclusion presents itself, and it doesn't please him one bit. The murders of the nun and the notary are connected; the crimes were committed by the same person. Worse, he is sure Isabel knows something about it, more than she has let on. But he can't believe, or doesn't dare to, that the lawyer could also be the murderer. No more than he can convince himself that she ordered the murders. And yet, the facts are there, and facts don't lie. Sister Marie-Carmen and Pedro De La Vega are linked by official papers dating back to 1946. A death certificate from a maternity ward in Madrid and an adoption request received the same day. The same day that Emilia Ferrer's son was born. That single date is all the proof Diego needs to know that Emilia told him the truth, that the child she delivered that day was very probably kidnapped, taken from her, and sold to another family like any ordinary merchandise. That date could be the perfect motive, too.

The way Diego Martin sees it is there is only one thing to do: ask Isabel flat out for an explanation. But he's going to have to be patient and wait until she returns from Paris. She must be grieving terribly for her grandmother; they were very close. That's what Isabel told him, that night they spent in Casa Pepe poring over the documents she brought to show him. But there is one problem: in this kind of situation, patience is not exactly his forte. Diego can demonstrate an almost Zen-like calm when an investigation demands it, but in his private life, he is an easily irritated hothead when he has to wait. And now, though he would never admit it, he is taking this investigation into a State scandal very personally. His attraction to Isabel, which he thinks must be mutual from the kiss she planted on the corner of his mouth, has thrown him for a loop in ways he never imagined possible anymore. As a result, he is examining his own motivations. Since he can't picture her having anything to do with the murders, is the reason because he doesn't want to? Because he wants to have a relationship with her? And if it turns out that she is involved, in any way, in the deaths of these two people, how will he react? Will it change his feelings for her? Yes, absolutely. But how?

He has a whole week ahead of him to continue his investigation and arrive at some answers. A week until Isabel is back in Madrid. A week to follow all the leads, examine all the possible hypotheses. For that, he needs Ana and her invaluable contacts among the cops and the intelligence agents. He knows she has a lot of work right now, but he needs to brainstorm with her. She has become closer to Isabel lately; maybe the lawyer told Ana things, insignificant things at first glance but that could shed light on some of the gray areas of his investigation.

When he finally does go to Ana with his suspicions, she is silent at first. Diego needed to get out of his apartment, so he came to see her at her office. As she listens to him talk, she occasionally knits her brow or shakes her head or scribbles some notes. Ana finally gets up, walks out from behind her desk, lights a cigarette, and flops down into her club chair with a long and profound sigh.

"Diego, you're killing me. I'm not convinced by what you're telling me, and yet if you look at the facts alone, your theory makes sense."

Silence. They stay like that for a long moment without speaking or even looking at each other, staring into space, lost in their thoughts, trying to digest everything they know and searching for ways to tie up loose ends. Right now, the main question they still have is "Why?" Ana can't stand not knowing. Before Diego can ask her to try to dig up some more information from the police and the intelligence agency, she picks up her phone and announces she is calling Ortiz at the CNI.

"At least then we'll know."

The call lasts just a few minutes. A meeting is discretely arranged for the following day. Ana thought she could hear a note of surprise in the voice on the other end of the line when she explained why she was calling. She hopes to have some answers in less than twenty-four hours. In the meantime, she'll put the finishing touches on the trap she is setting for the NASB's infiltrator, so he can never harm them again. She lays out her plan to Diego: as funny as he finds her idea, the Crusaders for Christ will certainly not be as amused.

Ana invites Diego to come with her. She needs to meet her prostitute friends to go over the final details, and she can't risk showing up late. Moreover, ever since the NASB's demonstration in the streets of Madrid, the atmosphere is electric. The country has practically split in two. Fringe groups like the Francoist throwbacks, traditionalist Catholics, and other reactionaries are starting to fight back. The NASB's website has been targeted numerous times by hackers, though unsuccessfully this time. The building housing the NASB's headquarters has been graffitied, and there are daily demonstrations outside by clean-shaven, buttoned-up protestors and by militants from different political and religious extremist groups who hurl insults and sometimes even tomatoes and eggs at anyone coming and going. They are spurred to ever more violent action with each passing day that the NASB's message gets greater traction with the population and the media, especially the international press. One morning, a truck filled with manure dumped its stinking load at the NASB's doorstep while the sickos applauded. A priest also came to recite the Hail Mary in Latin on his knees.

However, the resistance is becoming more coordinated too. Several organizations on the left—from political parties and labor unions to NGOs—have offered their support to the NASB to grow its members and train its staff. Help that is much needed. Regional chapters are opening in several cities, and, most notably, demonstrations are taking place, more or less spontaneously, on a daily basis. Zaragoza, A Coruña, Sevilla, Gijón, Salamanca, and other cities have each hosted a silent march. Even held midweek, each of these was attended by thousands of people. The movement is seriously ramping up. And, without fail, clashes disrupt the end of the marches. Pro- and anti-NASB militants are facing off in ever more violent confrontations. The police, meanwhile, are losing patience, sometimes firing indiscriminately at the protesters, leaving some seriously wounded. That was the case in Gijón. This city in northern Spain sits between a naval shipyard and a mining region and has long been at the epicenter of the country's largest protest movements (unsurprisingly, given its location), and its residents don't back down from anything. The silent march in Gijón took a violent turn when far-right militants looking for a fight were met by miners who were better-schooled at street brawling. But an eight-year-old kid lost an eye in the incident. A Flash-Ball fired at close range. The minister of justice was forced to resign. A diversion to defuse the situation, to make the people believe the government is listening to them, that it has the situation under control, and is responding accordingly.

A strategy, however, that is not pulling the wool over anyone's eyes. The last decision the minister of justice made before he resigned was to dismiss Judge David Ponce before the disciplinary board could even come back with a verdict. Fired, effective immediately. As for the inquiry that he opened into the stolen babies, it's safe to say it is now six feet under in the basement of the courthouse and locked up tight. If it seemed for a moment like everything could change, nothing, in fact, has changed. The political class is clinging to its privileges. And protecting the people who, one way or another, put them in power so that they can keep everything just as it is. "Status quo" is their motto. The Amnesty Law allowed them to slip through the fingers of the justice system, and they are not going to let a French lawyer who appeared out of the blue one day screw everything up for them. In the long run, they don't care if the story about kidnapped babies is true or not. The only thing that matters to them is that they continue to live as they always have. The economic crisis? They don't even know what that is, with their offshore accounts and their tax lawyers. Human trafficking of infants? What's to complain about if a few kids were adopted by well-to-do families?

Walking to Ana's appointment with her former colleagues, Diego tries to find out if Isabel ever told her anything. Nothing. Isabel told the detective a brief version of her grandmother's story without going into much detail or providing any names or dates. The journalist is disappointed. Ana notices and tries to change the topic of conversation: she doesn't like to see her friend like this. Invariably, however, their discussion always comes back to the two murders, their similarities, and their implications. Ana already admitted at her office that she thinks Diego's theory is possible, and it's probably true, though she still can't believe the lawyer is the mastermind behind the murders and is less sure that Isabel pulled the trigger herself in these execution-style killings.

Because that is what they are talking about, after all: executions, pure and simple, carried out the same way the mafia settles its scores. In any case, Ana wonders, to argue against his hypothesis, why should they limit their investigation to these two murders? Haven't there been others committed over the past few months that shared the same modus operandi and which could be related to these two?

"We'll have to find out what other cases the cops are looking into, especially any unsolved murders," Ana continues. "Well, wait, why not Paco Gómez's murder on the night of the elections? His father was in Franco's inner circle, don't forget. He was killed just like the other two."

"If that's a joke, it's not funny. If you're right, you're only confirming my theory. We ought to try to get our hands on the official report, just to see. It still seems to me that we've overlooked something in that case. . . . Perhaps the ballistics. Don't you have some way of getting the ballistics report? If the same weapon was used, we could be pretty sure it was the same murderer."

"Or murderess."

"That would be crazy! But even if it wasn't the same gun that was used to kill the notary, the nun, and, why not, the APM councilman too, that doesn't prove anything either."

They have arrived outside the front door of a nightclub. It is still closed in the middle of the afternoon, but at night, it has one of the hottest scenes in Madrid. The Arena is the headquarters of Madrid's transgender community. Ana buzzes, and the two friends quickly push open the door and slip inside. The club is dark at this hour, but Cumbia is playing on the sound system—a Caribbean techno mix from Colombia—and they can see that a few people are already waiting for them, seated on the club's red satin divans and armchairs and sipping cocktails. They exchange greetings and then get down to business. The music is cut, and the lights go up. They move two tables together, and Ana takes out her camera, a laptop, and several pictures of a man seated at a computer and walking in the street, as well as a map of the city marked in several places with a cross.

Ten days. Isabel has spent ten days in Paris. Far more than she ever imagined. To bury her grandmother, to be alone, to be far from the turmoil in Madrid. She needed time to step back for a moment. Time to realize as well that she misses Diego. She refused her parents' invitation to stay with them and found a comfortable hotel instead. She hasn't disconnected entirely from the news from Spain; she has checked in daily with one or another member of the NASB's executive committee. The movement has outgrown anything she ever imagined. But that only proves that she has been right all along, that the first handful of families who had been looking for their children for years, who never gave up, who always suspected the authorities had lied to them, who always believed their sons and daughters were still alive, were only the tip of the iceberg. Hundreds, even thousands, more families are bringing their cases, too. Everyone knows that people "disappeared" under dictatorships in Latin America. Now they will also know—Isabel is sure beyond a shadow of a doubt—that babies were abducted by the Franco regime. How many? If Spain wants to retain a shred of self-respect, it has no choice but to fully investigate this scandal. But the government seems unwilling to let the cat out of the bag.

Once back in Madrid, the lawyer hits the ground running. A quick visit to the NASB headquarters. Then a quick stop at home. And now back to the CNI. Before leaving for France, she had promised to return, to finish the conversation that began there. In the meantime, she has texted Ana and Diego to let them know she is back. Now Isabel is seated in the same windowless room as before, but she isn't as nervous as the first time. Before she boarded her flight in Paris, she had a minute to speak to Ana, who reassured her: Nicolás Ortiz, the chief of the CNI unit that is responsible for her surveillance, is a friend whom Isabel can trust as well. Ana also explained his limp, which forces him to walk with a cane. It is because of a bullet he took in the leg years ago during a tumultuous raid on an active ETA cell. When he arrives, Isabel shakes his hand, a gesture to let him know that she followed his advice and spoke to their mutual friend.

"Before we get started, my deepest condolences. I understand you were very close to your grandmother. Well, I didn't want to say too much the other day, but we really have to talk seriously about a few matters. Your security for one thing. As for the other, it's a little more problematic."

"I'm listening. But I can't help but wonder about your mysteriousness. What could be more problematic than death threats?"

A long silence. Then Ortiz launches into a lengthy monologue about why and how she was put under surveillance. The longer he talks, the more details he provides. And the more Isabel feels a noose tightening around her neck. They have been tracking her every move since the press conference announcing the creation of the NASB. She always suspected she would be on their radar but not exactly on a daily basis. She had told herself, of course, that the intelligence services would try to find out about her, but she never imagined two agents would be assigned to stick to her, 24/7, over several months. The government didn't spare any means or expense. And even though this Ortiz is one of Ana's friends, has a good reputation, and is considered to be on the political left, his reassurances that her surveillance was for her own safety and not performed with the intention of spying on her aren't putting her at ease.

His words are clear, precise, and direct. He outlines for her his team's various operations and discoveries of late, as the threats to her safety became more and more serious. Several far-right-identified organizations had her in their sights, not just the Crusaders for Christ. No surprise as to who has been behind the anonymous letters, the messages sent via social media and the Internet, and the insults, some of which were extremely violent. The Internet's anonymity gives people free reign to say the worst. They sorted through all of these, from the comments of run-of-the-mill reactionaries to the more carefully composed but no less sinister messages sent by a few genuine crazies. The CNI wire-tapped people close to certain religious and political organizations in the hope of heading off an attack by some brainwashed maniac. In particular, they kept a close eye on the headquarters of the Crusaders for Christ, but they had to be especially discrete about it, given the close ties between the CNI's director and traditional-ist Catholics.

Ortiz sums up by concluding that the risk to Isabel is very serious. She has already been the victim of a mostly harmless attack. The consequences of a future attack could be much worse. He does not propose to increase her protection, however. In fact, he never mentions that possibility at all.

So far, Isabel has listened to him attentively, without interrupt-ing him. However, this next part of his speech leaves her no choice but to react. Moreover, she is going to have to play a very careful game with Ortiz. What he is telling her now is that she is the leading suspect in several crimes.

"Let's be clear; I'm not charging you with anything for the moment. However, we have you on video surveillance footage not far from the parking structure where Pedro De La Vega was assassinated. We also know you were in Valencia the day Sister Marie-Carmen was murdered. And we were able to confirm that you had a train ticket for Barcelona the same day that the doctor Juan Ramírez was found dead in the street in the Gótico neigh-borhood. Finally, we have evidence that would put you in La Moraleja on the morning the president of the Mediterranean Sav-ings Bank took a bullet in the head during his morning jog."

Every new sentence pronounced by the CNI's unit chief hits her like a blow to the head. *Breathe. Don't panic. Think fast. Reveal nothing.* Isabel clears her throat before speaking.

"So you're accusing me of being a murderer, is that right?"

"No, as I just explained, I'm not accusing you of anything; I'm only sharing with you certain, shall we say, unfortunate coincidences between your schedule and some very serious facts. We are, after all, talking about the murders of several people. But I'm certain there is an explanation and that you can provide it for me now."

"I'm not going to tell you anything," Isabel states with resolve. "Everything you've just told me amounts to nothing more than conjecture. You don't have any proof."

"Very well, but as we speak, two of my agents are searching your apartment. Maybe what they turn up will make you change your mind. While we're waiting for their report, I'm going to ask you to wait here."

"You can't do that! How did they get in? On what grounds?"

"Madam, your security and that of the State are ample grounds to take liberties with the law. And never more so than in matters of life and death."

16

DAVID PONCE IS with Diego in their usual bar when the judge's dismissal is announced. Radio Uno's directors gave in to the pressure and are letting David continue his weekly justice report, especially since he refuses to be paid for it. The station could hardly say no to this now-famous public figure and to the ensuing free publicity. Diego and David are preparing the upcoming show when David's phone rings. The news hits him harder than expected, but he keeps up his spirits enough to buy everyone at Casa Pepe a round of drinks to celebrate what he insists on calling his "freedom." The two friends raise a toast to that and, after pausing a moment to let the news sink in, continue their discussion as if nothing happened. Well, almost nothing. To avoid interruptions, Ponce turns off his phone. He is in no mood to take calls from the media, nor is he under any obligation to make a public appearance or a statement, and that suits him just fine. The now ex-judge knows exactly what his next move will be. He had previously shared it with Diego to get his friend's opinion when David first learned of the disciplinary actions taken against him. Tomorrow, as soon as his registration papers go through, he will cross to the other side of the courtroom, from judgment to defense. He will become a lawyer. A court-appointed attorney, to get started. He'll decide later if he joins a firm (if anyone will have him) or if he starts his own (the most likely scenario).

For the time being, the question on the table is still the stolen babies. The scandal cost Ponce his job, it's true, but his decision to open the inquiry got him exactly what he wanted, on some unconscious level. He confides in Diego that he was getting tired of his job—the pressure, the endlessly accumulating cases, the scarcity of means at his disposal, the magistracy's close ties to politicians: "I think that, subconsciously, I opened the inquiry as a way of saying 'enough' without actually admitting it to myself. It allowed me to stop before I burned out."

As a future lawyer and a future colleague of Isabel Ferrer's, he disagrees emphatically with the journalist's theory. Ponce admits that there are quite a few similarities between these murders, but nothing supports Diego's conclusion that Isabel had a hand in any of it. Ana still hasn't spoken to her contact at the CNI, who has twice postponed a meeting. Ponce's advice is to wait for more information before accusing their young friend of anything. But Diego is annoyed precisely by the fact that Isabel seems to be avoiding him. He hasn't seen her since she got back from Paris, and they've hardly spoken on the telephone either, having just exchanged a few texts. It's as if she wants to cut off all ties with him. As if she suspects something is up. It would be foolish to think they became intimate friends over the course of a single night spent in a dive bar, but they both got caught up in the same cause and the same mess. Anyways, he'd just like to see her again. Until they have any more information, mainly from the CNI, he won't say anything to her. Still, he's sure she has changed somehow. For now, he figures it's just her grandmother's death or her heavy workload with the NASB. He really hopes that's all it is and nothing more.

It gets late, and Diego invites David back to his apartment: they'll smoke, drink some beers, and share a plate of cold cuts. The next radio show is going to be in a more usual vein—it won't be about the scandal—so that Diego almost feels as if he's on vacation. He's already written up the running order sheet and edited the main interview, this time with a Norwegian author he especially likes, Jo Nesbø, who writes the only crime novels to come out of Norway that Diego can actually understand. There are just a few last t's to cross, which amount to next to nothing. Even if the stolen babies story is far from finished and the country continues to tear itself to pieces over it, a break can't hurt, at least for one week. And so, *Radio Confidential* continues its regularly scheduled programming, before, very likely, returning to the attack in a future edition.

In another Madrid neighborhood, far from Diego's apartment in Malasaña, a man is seated on his couch, his head hanging as if he has fallen asleep watching television. If he could look out the window, he'd notice police lights. Several squad cars have taken up position in front of the building, and an ambulance is coming down the street, siren wailing. The man doesn't move. Uniformed police officers race up to the third floor and knock on the half-opened door. They call through the opening, ask if anyone is home, and if they can come in. No response. They arm themselves and enter the tiny two-room apartment. Facing them in the living room as they come through the door is the body of the NASB's volunteer computer programmer and militant in the Crusaders for Christ, who was also Isabel and Diego's assailant. His body is still warm. The neighbors called the police only ten minutes earlier, saying they heard a gunshot. At first, it looks like a suicide. But only at first.

When the crime squad and the forensics team arrive, they come immediately to the same conclusion. The man was murdered, but the scene was altered to resemble a suicide. Several elements give it away. The gun next to the victim's hand—the victim, they now know, is a certain Pablo Martínez, age thirty-two, born in Pamplona—could never have gotten there on its own. If he had killed himself, they would have found it on the floor. The body's position, seated on the couch, is also a dead giveaway. If he had shot himself in the head, the impact would have thrown him to one side. The traces of blood also indicate the shot was fired at very close range but from above him where he sat by a standing shooter. The investigators find a piece of paper with the words *"Forgive me"* written on it and placed on the coffee table, as well as several photos showing the victim participating in what looks like an S&M ritual with transvestites and transsexuals.

The authorities begin their search. The apartment is stuffed with religious statues (of different saints, the Virgin Mary, and Christ), and the walls are covered with black-and-white photographs of priests, crucifixes, lithographs, and framed texts in Latin. It could be a monk's cell, except for the photos on the coffee table. The bedroom is furnished with a single mattress on the floor and a desk holding a laptop, some brochures about the Crusaders for Christ, piles of papers, and some more photos: Isabel Ferrer from close-up, from far away, on the street, and in an office. A date and a time are scribbled on a Post-it, along with an ominous drawing of a skull-and-crossbones. In a drawer are a hunting knife, a semi-automatic pistol, and a full box of 9mm ammunition.

This is an unexpected development, so when the director of the crime squad gets the report from his men at the scene, he calls the CNI immediately. A memo had gone out after Isabel Ferrer was assaulted, instructing officers to report to the intelligence services if they found even the slightest evidence implicating Martínez in any way. Nicolás Ortiz arrives in person and asks the police to seal the crime scene. Meaning touch nothing and leave immediately. Only the forensics expert and the unit chief for the crime squad are allowed to remain. The CNI's agents get to work. Ortiz approaches the photos on the coffee table showing the victim surrounded by transvestites and transsexuals and then stops in his tracks. He leaves the apartment and gets Ana on the phone.

"We've got a problem," he tells her and explains that the computer programmer is dead.

"Shit! That wasn't supposed to happen," Ana says with shock. "What are you going to do?"

"We've taken over the investigation, so it should be all right. This would be a good time to pay a visit to the Crusaders for Christ. In my opinion, they're the ones behind this. They couldn't stand to see the photos you sent them. It's a long way from there to bumping off the guy, I'll admit. I wasn't expecting this. But it proves one thing: they've got a bad case of nerves, and they're capable of almost anything. Isabel Ferrer is in grave danger. She is clearly their next target. I'm going to step up her protection and call her back into headquarters."

"OK, let me know what happens. I'll be in touch."

This time, it is a formal summons that Isabel receives. The courtesy calls are over. Even if her last visit to the CNI ended rather badly and she slammed the door on her way out, she was free to leave. She was unsettled by what Ortiz knew about the murders of the notary and the nun and surprised to learn he found out about her trip to Barcelona and the doctor's death. Isabel feels certain he knows more than he is letting on, which worries her a bit. Now she is being escorted by three agents—none of whom was assigned to her original surveillance—who have come for her at the offices of the NASB and are driving her back to CNI headquarters. They wouldn't tell her anything, but one of them served her a yellow paper summoning her to their office for questioning in a case. No further information. She follows them out under the astonished gaze of the association's volunteers, whom she tried to reassure as she prepared to leave by telling them not to worry and that she would be back soon. Isabel and the officers get into an unmarked car, and the gray delivery van starts up behind them as they pull away from the curb. In less than five minutes, the convoy arrives at its destination. Then it's the same thing all over again. The windowless basement room. And a long wait.

A young woman enters and offers Isabel a coffee and a sandwich, but she refuses to eat. The woman turns to leave, then changes her mind and walks back toward the lawyer. She puts one hand on her shoulder, bends down close to her face, and congratulates her for everything she has done. Then she leaves, closing the door softly behind her. Surprised, Isabel wonders if the woman's action wasn't part of a script, a ploy designed to put her at ease. She doesn't have long to think it over before Ortiz enters. His face is drawn. Before Isabel has a chance to say anything or ask if she is going to be held in custody, he places on the table an envelope from which he removes a pile of photos taken from the computer programmer's apartment and spreads them out in front of her.

"Hello, Isabel. I apologize for ordering you in so abruptly, but given how our last conversation ended, I thought it would be simpler to send my men for you," he begins. "There have been some new developments, and it's imperative that we talk, plainly this time."

He announces that the NASB's computer programmer has been murdered and that he was her assailant as well.

"The rat was there all along. . . . I suppose he was the one who stole the association's contact list, too. But why am I here? I have nothing to do with his death, I hope you don't imagine it was me who—"

"No, no, we already have an idea who is behind this, which is why I wanted to bring you in right away. You are the primary target of the Crusaders for Christ. We found evidence in the victim's apartment that they have been planning your murder. They radicalized some time ago, and they're looking for any means possible to get themselves on the map and steal attention from their more powerful rival, Opus Dei. Killing the spokesperson of the families whose children were kidnapped by the Franco regime would bring them unprecedented publicity."

Isabel takes the news hard. She always knew there could be risks for her if she took up the case of the stolen babies; she was aware of the danger, and she never ran from the possibility. But, no, getting shot, she never imagined it could come to that. It's beyond her worst nightmares. Threats she can deal with. The assault she handled well enough. But a murder attempt, by Catholic fundamentalists no less . . . *Shit*, she thinks to herself, *the country has gone completely off its rocker.*

"Well, now that you know, it's time to make a decision," Ortiz continues. "I'm going to offer you a deal, but no one outside of this room can know about it. For my part, I give you my word."

Nicolás Ortiz is taking a big risk. An enormous risk even. A carefully considered decision that cost him a few nights of sleep. He knows he's putting his neck on the block if his superiors ever discover what he is about to do. He trusts his men, but people can change loyalties. Over the course of his long career, he has never had to confront a moral dilemma such as the one he is facing now. He weighed the pros and cons, he went back to the beginning, and he examined them again, and then he made his choice. By listening to his heart more than his head, to the man he is, a Socialist, and not to the cop he became by training. It was difficult to make up his mind, but once he did, he looked at himself in the mirror and smiled. He hasn't smiled in a very long time. It convinced him that he made the right choice. And that if things go wrong, he will be ready to take the blame. And he won't regret a thing.

His offer leaves Isabel speechless. The truth is she hardly has any choice in the matter. She manages to thank him for being sensitive enough to her situation to give her a week to make up her mind and for stepping up her protection in the meantime by putting the two agents in the gray van at her disposition. Ortiz is certain that the Crusaders for Christ will waste no time in recruiting another assassin to put their plan into action.

She is already ninety-nine percent sure what her decision will be, but, for appearances' sake, she asks for time to think about it. She is going to have to act fast, find a way out of the NASB, and appoint a proper replacement as president. If she doesn't, Isabel will have nothing but trouble, the kind that will get her thrown into prison. The agents who searched her apartment found documents and weapons. Enough proof to convince Ortiz of her involvement in the five murders. She doesn't understand why he is making her this offer when he has everything he needs to have her arrested. Or perhaps she does understand, perfectly. He knows the government will do everything in its power to prevent the families from getting the answers they are demanding, and the Amnesty Law will never be overturned, that all of their complaints will be rejected by the courts and that justice will never be done. Perhaps this former anti-Franco militant and Socialist tells himself that, after all that has happened, Isabel's victims only got what they deserved. That it was a dirty job, but someone had to do it so that an old score could finally be settled with history.

It's been quite a week, in so many ways. The dramatic arrest of the hardcore leadership of the Crusaders for Christ has set off a torrent of reactions across the political spectrum. Surprised by this latest development and trying unsuccessfully to maintain a semblance of sangfroid, the government is on the defensive, a position the Socialists in the opposition are playing to their advantage by attacking wherever they can. A cardinal, a bishop, and several priests have been charged with conspiracy, attempted murder, and engaging in organized criminal activity. As fanatical, dangerous, and sectarian as the Crusaders for Christ are, the group emerged from within Opus Dei, and so the Catholic Church in Spain has unanimously condemned their treatment: arrested, handcuffed, and scheduled for trial as common criminals. When your brothers-in-arms are up shit creek, you have to stick together, no matter what your differences might be. All told, twenty arrests have been made. In addition to the prelates, the accused include several nuns, leaders from the business community, various employees in different ministries (Justice, Health, and Foreign Affairs, no less), and some parliamentary assistants. Half of those have been placed in detention pending trials, and the rest have been released on bail.

The press has had a field day with this unexpected turn of events in the stolen babies case. This time, much of the reporting has been sympathetic to Isabel Ferrer. Similarly, the ongoing demonstrations by families and members of the NASB have turned into rallies in support of its president. Ever since the press broke the news of the existence of the Crusaders for Christ, the country has been utterly stunned. The CNI is equally dumb-founded. Nicolás Ortiz, who led the investigation from its beginning, cannot believe the kind of organization the CNI managed to bring down. A sort of religious cartel, in fact. With the same pyramid-like structure favored by drug traffickers and the mafia. All members of the Crusaders of Christ must pledge a percentage of their salaries to the group. A seamlessly organized racket, as revealed by accounting files seized during the investigation. But what was the most screwball, even the most outrageous, aspect of the group? Everyone had a code name: CC1 for the leader, CC2, CC3, and so on down the line, depending on one's place in the hierarchy. The computer programmer, Pablo Martínez, was

CC189. The investigation is only getting underway, but it is already apparent that the Crusaders for Christ had nearly eight hundred members in its ranks.

Diego hasn't missed a beat. The revelations will obviously be the topic of an upcoming show. He and Ana were glued to the television for hours. Ortiz had given the private detective a heads-up that something was going down, but he didn't let on as to the size and importance of what was called Operation CC. Ortiz was too busy planning the police presence and surveillance on the Crusaders for Christ to keep their appointment, but he also didn't want to tell her anything concerning Isabel on the phone. So Ana and Diego are still in the dark on that subject. The only thing Ortiz let slip was that the lawyer had accepted an offer he made and that Isabel would tell them about it herself. He doesn't want to get involved in their friendship, and anyways, it's up to her to tell them or not. Despite Ana's insistence, he said no more than that.

For her part, Isabel has not been following the news. She has a few more loose ends to tie up before she leaves. Isabel had no choice but to say yes to Ortiz. It was either that or a trial and a prison sentence for committing five murders in the first degree. Suffice it to say she would have spent the rest of her life behind bars, she never would have come out alive, and the NASB would have been irreparably damaged. It's to save herself, of course, but also in the best interests of all of the families she hoped to defend that she has made the decision to leave the country. Her suitcases are packed, a real estate agency will find a renter for her apartment, which will provide a small but regular income until she gets on her feet, and her files are in a secure storage locker that only she knows about. All that's left to do is say goodbye: to the members of the NASB, but also to Diego, David Ponce, and Ana, all of whom she is meeting for dinner. And there is one other thing. For that, she has asked Ana to accompany her.

The two women haven't seen each other since Isabel's return from France, and Isabel is somewhat apprehensive at the idea of meeting the private detective again. She could hear it in Ana's voice when she called her—how hurt Ana is that Isabel waited this long to get in touch. She apologized and promised to explain everything later that evening at Casa Pepe. Isabel has already gone to the bar to ask the owner if he would agree to close the place early one more time. For her. For Diego. For David. For Ana. He agreed begrudgingly, but his complaints were only for show. The truth is he could never say no to something for Diego. Everyone will gather there at ten o'clock that night. No one but Isabel knows that this will be a rather unusual dinner. She asked Ana to meet her at eight o'clock. Two hours should be plenty of time to do what she needs to do. Isabel has filled a large cardboard box with five thick file folders. The ones that are numbered. The ones containing the information she gathered on her five victims. She closed the box, sealed it with packing tape, and put it in the trunk of her car.

The detective is right on time. Ana seems reserved but otherwise happy to see Isabel again. Their destination is the Casa de Campo, Madrid's largest public park. The former hunting grounds of the royal family are now a public park stretching thousands of acres in the west of the city. At night, the area is known to be frequented by prostitutes and drug dealers, but families flock here in the daytime for its zoo, its lake, and its amusement park. The sun has not yet set when they arrive. Isabel hasn't told Ana why they are there, and the silence in the car is oppressive as Isabel finds a place to park at the entrance. Joggers and parents pushing strollers pass by, as do the first prostitutes of the evening. It's that time of day when two worlds, day and night, overlap. Isabel asks Ana to help her carry the box; it isn't particularly heavy, but it's a conversation opener.

"What the hell are we doing here? What is this thing? What's in it?" The private detective sounds annoyed.

"They're files that I want to burn: papers and old documents that I don't need anymore."

"And we had to come here to do it? You couldn't have simply bought a paper shredder?"

"Give me a hand instead of complaining."

Isabel moves the carton a little way from them and then removes from her backpack a small shovel and a bottle of denatured alcohol as Ana watches in astonishment. Two CNI agents are looking on from a distance and wondering too why Isabel has led them there. After checking that the hole is deep enough, she pushes the box in and pours the alcohol over it. Then she lights a cigarette, takes a few drags, and throws it in the hole. The box goes up in a blaze of orange flames. The two women watch it burn. For the twenty minutes it takes for the fire to extinguish itself, Isabel tells Ana about her grandmother and what happened to her, about her grandfather too, why Isabel left France to come to Madrid, and why she became involved with the NASB. Crying now as ashes from the fire blow around them, she finishes her story.

"I'm leaving."

"What? Where?"

Ana listens to Isabel's story, expecting Isabel at any moment to tell her something that would confirm or disprove Diego's theory, but she never does. Nothing. And Ana is stupefied by the last thing she hears Isabel say.

"Don't ask me anything, please. I'll tell you everything, but I want Diego to be there when I do. I owe you both an explanation, and I'm going to give it to you. I'm a little afraid of how you'll take it, and, above all, I'm not sure if I should tell you in front of David—"

"Dammit, you're scaring the shit out of me! Go on, tell me what this is all about!"

"Let's go back to the car. If you drive, I'll see if I can find the words to tell you."

Ana drives, and Isabel talks. About the nun. And the notary. Ana can't believe what she is hearing. Diego was right. She has to pull over in the emergency lane of Madrid's beltway to take it all in. She is having difficulty breathing. She calms down, tries to think clearly. But she can't control her reaction. It's impossible to be angry with Isabel. True, she killed five people, but Ana cannot bring herself to judge her and doesn't want to either. Instead, she understands what Isabel did and realizes that she, too, could have done the same thing. And that frightens Ana. Doesn't she always say that if she ever crossed paths with the man who tortured her in an Argentine prison that she would kill him with her bare hands? Another worry is Diego. She has no idea how he is going to take the news. As for David, Isabel is right: he can't know anything. The ex-judge has too much respect for justice and seeing it carried out. He wouldn't do anything or denounce Isabel, of course, but he would refuse to have anything more to do with her. Or with Ana either, for that matter. When they get back to Isabel's building, the two go upstairs to wash up and make themselves more presentable. They still have thirty minutes until they have to meet the men. Ana could also use a stiff drink.

When they knock on the roll-down gate at Casa Pepe, Diego and David are already there. The journalist and the ex-judge are in high spirits and have already opened a bottle. They are celebrating the demise of those raving lunatics, the Crusaders for Christ, and they are pleased to see the detective and the lawyer. Ana is as white as a sheet, and Isabel can only manage a forced smile. They make a brave show of gaiety and don't let on to the two men that their mood is far gloomier than theirs. Ponce immediately plants a kiss on Isabel with the express intention of provoking her.

"We don't have to be so formal anymore now that we're colleagues!"

He also announces that he'll probably have to leave early since he is on duty tonight. As for Diego, he is trying to hide his delight at seeing Isabel again.

"So tell us, you really didn't want to see us or what?" he asks, pouring Isabel a glass of red wine. "How are you doing after everything that's happened?"

"OK, I'm holding up. I've had so much work that I haven't had a minute to myself. I'm happy to see you all again, and I've wanted to thank you for everything you did for the association and for me."

"Sounds like a eulogy," David exclaims, still teasing Isabel when his phone rings. "Yeah, it's me. OK, I'm on my way. I'll be there in twenty minutes." He lets out a long sigh. "Well, I'm going to have to leave you; I've got a client waiting for me. A small-time dealer in the neighborhood."

Isabel shoots a look at Ana, who gets her meaning and answers with a discreet nod. She already persuaded Isabel not to say anything to David about her five victims; only to let him know that she will be leaving for her safety. The lawyer has something else to tell him, though.

"David, before you go, I have something to tell the three of you. It's just that . . . I'm going away, I'm leaving the country. The threats have become too serious. They want to kill me, and they'll succeed if I stay here. I don't want to live my life like Saviano* or like those people who have to have permanent police protection, a cop at my back all the time. I could never put up with that. The CNI has taken care of everything. They're going to exfiltrate me, sort of, and make sure I leave the country while I can still walk and I'm in good health."

---

*Italian investigative journalist and author who wrote about the Naples mafia and who lives under police protection.

Complete silence. Isabel's announcement has taken the wind out of the men's sails. No more kidding around. The journalist feels completely let down. The ex-judge doesn't know what to say. David's expected any minute at the police station, but he doesn't really want to leave anymore. Still, he has to. As he's getting ready to go, the lawyer stops him.

"Wait!"

She walks over to him and hands him a key and a tiny piece of paper.

"Here, take this. This is for the storage unit where I've left all of the files on the families in the NASB. Keep them for me. I trust you. I'm sure you'll know what to do with them."

"I promise. Take good care of yourself. And let us know how you're doing. Well, I have to go, or my client's not going to be happy!"

Seated on a bar stool, Diego still hasn't said a word. He thinks Isabel's running away, and he wants an explanation. He is trying to calm himself before his anger gets the better of him. One thing is for sure: no one feels like eating the tapas that the owner left for them. The bottles of wine, on the other hand, aren't going to last long. Lost in his thoughts, he doesn't hear Isabel sit down next to him. She puts her hand on his arm. He jumps. Ana is watching them out of the corner of her eye from where she has slumped onto a banquette.

"When are you leaving?" Diego asks.

"Tomorrow."

"Where?"

"Far. Far from Madrid. Far from Spain. Far from France."

"Yes, but where?"

"I'm not able to tell you that now."

Irritated by what he interprets as a lack of trust in him, Diego removes his arm, gets up, and pours himself another glass of wine. Then he begins.

"Do you plan to come back someday?"

"I have no idea right now. I hope so. It's a forced exile, but it isn't permanent. Or at least I hope not."

"So this is a goodbye dinner that you've planned?"

"Yes, in a way. It's also something that I have been dreading because I have some things to tell you. It's a story that I started to tell Ana on our way here, but I'd like to start over from the beginning. Before I do, just promise to hear me out: no questions or interruptions."

No answer from Diego. He passes one hand across his face. He feels trapped, betrayed almost, by someone he trusted, someone he respected, whose determination and courage he admired. And the first woman for whom he has felt something besides sympathy since the death of his beloved Carolina.

"Promise me," Isabel repeats.

"All right, if you insist. Go on, I'm listening."

They sit down next to Ana, who now draws herself up straight and pushes the plates of chorizo and ham out of the way. She fills everyone's glasses. Isabel takes a long drink, then dives in. She confesses everything, speaking slowly, sometimes searching for the right words, occasionally stopping to take a sip of some of that red liquid that she loves so much. She tells them everything, right down to the last detail. It takes a whole hour. Diego is champing at the bit and sometimes expels deep breaths of air like a bull about to enter the ring.

As she describes the murders, she relives every moment of them. The APM official the night of the elections, who was the first. The terror of being caught. The fear that she could miss and lose her shot at him. The notary: she talked to him, he replied, and then a second later, she took his life with no remorse. The doctor: that one was quicker, and no words were exchanged. The banker: more complicated, and with a long wait; it seemed almost surreal to her because he was so far away when he fell. And the nun finally: the riskiest one of all, a woman in a religious sanctuary in the middle of a street festival. As she continues to talk, Ana and Diego find it increasingly difficult to contain their shock and to remain seated and not interrupt her with a thousand questions. But every time, as if she could read their thoughts, she stays one step ahead of them. The journalist can barely contain himself. He smokes cigarette after cigarette, clenches his fists, and clamps his teeth so hard his gums start to bleed. Finally, she explains why.

"When my grandfather died, my grandmother, Emilia, was inconsolable. For weeks, she never stopped crying. I went to see her every day, anytime I could get away. One evening, it was just the two of us, and we were looking at old photos. I don't know why I thought of it, but I asked her if she ever regretted that they never went back to Spain after living so long in France. I was telling her that the dictatorship was over, that the country had changed, and the past was in the past, but her answer was 'Never!' And then she told me the whole story. She explained what their lives were like as anti-Franco militants: the deprivation, the repression, and friends imprisoned and murdered. But despite all that, they loved each other, and they decided to start a family. The story of her delivery and the loss of her baby devastated me. One thing led to another, and we got onto the subject of forgiveness, and then revenge. We stayed up all night talking. Early in the morning, I went out to get some croissants for breakfast. When I came back, she was still in her chair. She hadn't moved, but she looked different, as if a weight had been taken from her. I made us some coffee, and we ate, and then she told me about her idea, her plan. She was so convinced that she would never have justice, nor would any of the other families who lost their children. She knew there were other families, other women who had known the same wrenching pain of having their babies taken from them by people with no morals or scruples. She asked me to put her plan for revenge into action. But she didn't just want revenge, she wanted me, as a lawyer, to get behind the cause and help victims like herself. I started to look into it, discreetly. I found quite a lot of information that confirmed what she told me. I started to realize that a whole system, the scope of which I didn't quite grasp back then, had been created to abduct the children of families in the political opposition and sell them to families who might not have been open Franco supporters yet who shared in any case a certain number of the regime's ideas. I had the name of the nun. From there, I worked backwards and found the names of everyone else involved. The doctor, the nun, the banker, the politician, the notary. Each of them was a link in the chain. I had to eliminate them all, one after the other. To be free of the past. That's it. Now you know everything."

Ana has been crying for some time. It's even worse than she imagined. Ana and Diego had figured out the connection between two of the murders, but there were five in all. Despite everything Isabel did, Ana can't bring herself to hate her. Isabel's story is deeply moving. Of course, Ana knows that no one has the right to take justice into their own hands, that Isabel went too far, and she is a murderer. Still, Ana doesn't give a damn. She can understand where Isabel's coming from. Diego has not said a word. Isabel is waiting for a reaction. Afraid of what it might be. With good reason. He looks at her with daggers in his eyes, then picks up his empty glass and throws it against the wall. He stands up, grabs his chair, and hurls it to the floor. Then he leaves without another word. Outside, he begins walking wherever the streets take him. He walks. He walks all night. He cries, too. Franco is dead, but not the evil he brought into the world.

EPILOGUE

IT HAS BEEN nine months since Isabel left. Nine months since Diego has had any contact with her. After his sudden departure from the bar that night, and after having accepted, for good or bad, what she told them, it still took him weeks to get over it. He still feels like he was played by the lawyer. Above all, he can't understand her or find any excuse that would justify what she did. She killed five people in cold blood. She pulled the trigger on human lives. Premeditated, deliberate, planned murders. Certainly, her victims did not have clean consciences themselves. But even if they inflicted the worst suffering that anyone can on a woman who has just given birth, they didn't deserve to die. And two of them paid for the actions of others: they were targets by default. The APM councilman and the banker were murdered as the "sons of." The bullets that ripped through their skulls were destined for their fathers. But since they were already dead, she punished the sons. They paid with their lives for the sins of their fathers. No matter what happened to her grandmother, Diego can't bear the idea that Isabel became a vigilante and that she debased herself to commit an irreparable crime, five times.

Isabel is gone, but the scandal is not over. On the contrary, her departure only heightened the drama. And Diego is still following the story assiduously. Every month, he dedicates one episode of *Radio Confidential* to the stolen babies scandal. An unprecedented wave of protests rocked the country, but the government is still standing. It even used the current context to pass legislation to crack down on public demonstrations and gatherings, which says it all. Also, the investigation was dropped, of course, but with the help of David Ponce as its new legal counsel, the NASB has taken its case to the European Court of Human Rights, which ordered the Ministry of Justice to reopen an investigation. A victory for the former magistrate, who could hardly refuse to take up Isabel's mantle. When he opened the storage locker with the key she gave him, David felt sick to his stomach. All of her archives were there. Dozens and dozens of files. He read them all. An entire month was spent that way, and he hardly ever left his apartment except to return to the storage locker for more. One morning, he showed up at the NASB's offices.

"Hi, I'm your new lawyer."

Since that day, David has spared no effort to help families get answers to their questions. That much, at least. As for who should bear the blame, that's a more complicated question. This system of child trafficking that began under the dictatorship lasted for years; just bringing all the facts to light won't be easy. Moreover, it's highly unlikely that the case will ever come to trial. So he makes it his fight, every day, to speak out so that all of these horrific stories are told.

David's regular appearances on Diego's radio show have proved an effective platform for ensuring that this part of Spain's recent history will not be forgotten. Diego, too, has thrown himself into the cause. He has just published a book, *¿Donde están?* (*Where are they?*), which jumped immediately to number one on the best-seller list. In it, he connects the dots between the stolen babies and the five assassinations, but he never exposes Isabel's involvement. He argues that it is highly probable that one and the same person committed all five murders, but he also makes it clear that he does not know who pulled the trigger or who ordered the killings. It's a lie by omission that he decided on after lengthy discussions with Ana. The detective convinced him to write a book on the subject. She encouraged him and supported him throughout the writing process. She also pushed him to change his initial course, which was to name Isabel as the murderer, so that he finally backed down. Ana won the argument by invoking the question of vengeance. "When Carolina was murdered, you swore to me right away that you wanted to find her assassins and kill them yourself, so they'd end up the same way," she reminded him. He still doesn't have an explanation for why Isabel did what she did, but he decided finally not to add fire to the flame by doing her more harm than she has already done to herself. In any case, she is paying dearly for it now. A forced exile, with no date on the horizon for her eventual return.

It was Ana who drove Isabel to the airport the day after their tumultuous goodbye dinner. Before Isabel passed through security on the way to her gate, she gave Ana a letter to deliver to

Diego. He never opened it. It sits on his desk; he looks at it every day, without knowing if he will ever have the courage to read it.

As if she were defying history itself, Isabel went to Argentina. Another country that has survived its own years of dictatorship, abductions, and stolen babies. She chose to go to Buenos Aires, the most European of Latin American cities. She felt at home as soon as she arrived. She got settled discreetly. The two CNI agents were seated not far from her during the fourteen-hour trip and followed her wherever she went. That is until she found an apartment in the Palermo district and they were sure she was no longer in any danger. During those first weeks, she walked everywhere, soaking up the atmosphere of her adopted city, its streets, its odors, its lifestyle, and its music, too. She visited its museums and spent time in its bars and its *milongas*, learning to dance the tango. She read a lot and thought a lot. About what she did, the consequences of her actions, and what she planned to do next. She waited for a response from Diego, but none ever came. A sign from him. A message. A call. And then she gave up hoping he would contact her, that they would be able to talk, that she could explain her motivations and her reasons. She had to look for work too. She didn't have much difficulty finding a job. A phone call and an appointment were enough. For the last three months, she has been working as a legal advisor for the Mothers of the Plaza de Mayo. They are also looking for their children and grandchildren who "disappeared" under a dictatorship.

●

ACKNOWLEDGMENTS

A writer writes alone. Alone in front of the empty page of a note-book that he hopes to fill with words that will make sense. Alone in front of a computer screen and a document that waits for his fingers to fly over the keyboard. Alone with himself as well. But the fact is that a writer is not truly alone when he sits down to write. As I sit to write these acknowledgments, memories flood back of the people who, consciously or unconsciously, were with me as I wrote. The first memories that come to mind are of the times I spent with my grandparents in Spain. They told me about their lives during the Franco years and their involuntary depar-ture for France, and without them, I would never have had the idea to undertake this story. My parents inculcated in my sister and me a belief in our great fortune to have two cultures. I am French. I am Spanish. I don't want to have to choose between them. For that and for everything else, gracias. I hope I will mea-sure up and that I may pass the torch to my own children, Léa and Diego.

This book took root in my imagination several years ago. Then I had to get the project started, commit to it, and begin. Write, read, and reread. And ask others to read it too. I must mention here my two exceptional editors, two superwomen: Tiffany Gassouk and Anik Lapointe. In Paris and in Barcelona, they pushed, encouraged, and advised me. My profound thanks to both of them. I would also like to thank Véronique Cardi, director of the collection Livre de Poche, who had the courage and the excellent idea to launch "Préludes" and to make a place for my novel there.

So many other friends deserve recognition here, but I'm afraid of making a blunder and forgetting any of them. However, I cannot finish without a nod to Manu Chao for the title of the novel, of course, but for his friendship too. I hope that I did as you asked and made good use of "*Mala Vida.*"

Finally, and perhaps more than anybody else, two people deserve to be remembered in these pages, as they have my deepest gratitude. Paolo Bevilacqua, my friend and travel companion, who was by my side throughout the writing of this book. His enthusiasm, his encouragement, and his sense of humor every day in the offices of the magazine *Alibi* were invaluable to me. Thanks for putting up with me. And Sophie, my Sophie. Words fail me. You were my first reader, of course, my unconditional support, and the source of my inspiration and my motivation. Without you, I would never have succeeded. Without you, nothing is ever possible.